"Alone At Last."

Roark came up behind her, his breath warm and provocative against her neck.

"I think our engagement party was a success." Was that her sounding breathy and turned on? All night she'd been swamped with the longing to feel his hands on her.

"We achieved what we set out to do. The auction house board knows that beauty has tamed the beast."

Despite the way his fingers wandered along her waist with turbulent results, Elizabeth chuckled. "I think I'd characterize you more like the big bad wolf."

He spun her around so abruptly her mouth opened in a startled huff.

"Then prepare to be gobbled up."

She knew this was what she needed to guard against. But then his lips captured hers, robbing her of breath, torching her senses, and a wave of longing crashed into her, drowning all thought....

Dear Reader,

I was so thrilled to be asked to be part of The Highest
Bidder continuity. I've always thought auction houses
were glamorous and exciting. What a huge thrill to see
something you want, and to have to bid against other
equally interested competitors. Higher and higher the
price goes. Where do you draw the line between wanting
something and the price you'll have to pay to get it?

It's a question that plagues Elizabeth Minerva as she finds
herself torn between her longing to be a mother and her
love for billionaire adventurer Roark Black—a man who
blows into New York City every few months to wow
everyone with his latest antiquities find and stir up the
social scene before he's off on his next quest. She can't
have both.

Like Roark, I'm very interested in ancient history, and
I had a blast discovering all sorts of interesting stories
while researching Middle Eastern artifacts.

The Rogue's Fortune was a hard book to stop working on.
Elizabeth and Roark were fascinating characters, and long
after the book was finished I kept imagining them in all
sorts of adventures together. I hope you enjoy their story.

All the best!

Cat Schield

CAT SCHIELD

THE ROGUE'S FORTUNE

HARLEQUIN®
entertain, enrich, inspire™

Special thanks and acknowledgment to Cat Schield
for her contribution to The Highest Bidder miniseries.

Recycling programs
for this product may
not exist in your area.

ISBN-13: 978-0-373-73205-0

THE ROGUE'S FORTUNE

Printed in U.S.A.

Books by Cat Schield

Harlequin Desire

Meddling with a Millionaire #2094
A Win-Win Proposition #2116
Unfinished Business #2153
The Rogue's Fortune #2192

Other titles by this author available in ebook format.

CAT SCHIELD

has been reading and writing romance since high school. Although she graduated from college with a B.A. in business, her idea of a perfect career was writing books for Harlequin. And now, after winning the Romance Writers of America 2010 Golden Heart Award for series contemporary romance, that dream has come true. Cat lives in Minnesota with her daughter, Emily, and their Burmese cat. When she's not writing sexy, romantic stories for Harlequin Desire, she can be found sailing with friends on the St. Croix River or in more exotic locales like the Caribbean and Europe. She loves to hear from readers. Find her at www.catschield.com. Follow her on Twitter @catschield.

To my Aunt Sophie

* * *

The Highest Bidder
*At this high-stakes auction house,
where everything is for sale,
true love is priceless.*

Don't miss a single story in this new continuity
from Harlequin Desire!

One

He sauntered through the well-dressed crowd, bestowing his lazy smile on those who gushed their congratulations. Tall and powerfully built, he'd been ogled by half the women he'd passed. He, in turn, seemed uninterested in the stir he created as he charmed his way through the two hundred guests assembled for the premier wine auction.

As he scanned the room like a secret service agent, only his penetrating eyes gave away the fact that he wasn't as relaxed as he appeared.

Most people wouldn't have noticed Roark Black was on edge. Most people didn't have super-sensitive radar for the dangerous types.

Elizabeth Minerva did.

"The shrimp is running out!"

Jolted out of her ruminating by Brenda Stuart, her quick-to-panic "assistant" on this event, Elizabeth ripped her gaze away from the handsome adventurer and skimmed damp palms from her waist to her hips.

"I just checked and there's plenty of shrimp left," Elizabeth told Brenda. Annoyance with herself fed her impatient tone. There was also plenty of champagne and canapés and a dozen other things Brenda had fussed about in the last hour. "Why don't you make yourself a plate and go relax in the back?"

Anything to get rid of the former wedding planner to the middle class. Josie Summers, Elizabeth's boss, had saddled her with Brenda because as always Josie had underestimated what Elizabeth could handle. It was the woman's second event as Elizabeth's second in command, and rubbing elbows with Manhattan's rich and famous was spotlighting exactly why Brenda wasn't ready to be here. Instead of projecting a confident, capable vibe as she moved invisibly through the party, Elizabeth's assistant had badgered a server in front of Bunny Cromwell, one of the city's most prolific hostesses, and scolded a bartender for not making a city councilman's drink properly.

"I can't relax," Brenda exclaimed, her sharp tone catching the attention of two nearby guests. The women exchanged disgusted expressions. "And you shouldn't either."

Plastering on a serene smile, Elizabeth seized Brenda's arm above the elbow, fingers pinching ever so delicately. "I've got everything under control here. The auction will be starting in a half an hour. Why don't you head home?"

"I can't." Brenda resisted Elizabeth's grip as she was hauled toward the screens set up at one end of the enormous loft space to conceal the food prep area from the party-goers.

"Sure, you can." Elizabeth used her soothing voice as she marched the older woman away from the party. "You've put in so many hours this week. You deserve to get out of here. I can handle the rest."

"If you're sure."

As if Elizabeth hadn't handled larger parties in the three years since she'd graduated from college and taken a job with Josie Summers's Event Planning. Granted, this was Elizabeth's first A-list crowd. The first event that had given her butterflies before the guests arrived and began to murmur their approval over the way she'd transformed a dull, empty loft space into a sophisticated, elegant venue.

"I'm positive," Elizabeth said. "Go home and tuck your beautiful daughter into bed."

It was well past ten and Brenda's six-year-old daughter was probably already fast asleep, but Elizabeth had figured out the first day she'd worked with the woman that everything Brenda did was for her little girl. It was the only thing about the woman Elizabeth liked. And envied.

"Okay. Thanks."

Elizabeth waited until Brenda had gathered her purse and disappeared down the long hallway toward the elevator before she headed back to the party.

"Well, hello."

She'd almost managed to forget about Roark Black in the ten minutes she'd been dealing with Brenda, but here he was, less than five feet away, leaning his broad shoulder against one of the two-foot-wide columns that supported the ceiling.

Damn. Up close the energy of the man was astonishing. He practically oozed lusty masculinity and danger. He'd forgone the traditional bow tie with his tux and left the top buttons undone on his white shirt. Rakish and sexy, he set her pulse to purring.

You swore off bad boys forever, remember?

And Roark Black was as bad a bad boy as they got. Even his name gave her the shivers.

Yet earlier, there she'd stood, daydreaming about what it would be like to slide her fingers through his thick wavy hair. Brown in color, the shade reminded her of her great aunt's sheared beaver coat. She'd loved the sensual drag of the soft fur against her bare skin.

"Can I get you something?" she asked.

One side of his mouth lifted. "I thought you'd never ask."

His tone invited her to smile at his flirting. His eyes dared her to strip off her black dress and give him a glimpse of what lay beneath.

She swallowed hard. "Is there something you need?" The second the question passed her lips, she wished it back. Was she trying to play into his hands?

"Sweetheart—"

"Elizabeth." She shoved out her hand all professional like. "Elizabeth Minerva. I'm your event planner."

She expected him to take her hand in a bone-crushing grip. Instead, he cupped it, turned her palm upward and dragged his left forefinger down the middle of it. Her body went on full alert like a state penitentiary with a missing prisoner.

"Roark." He peered at her palm, the skin glazed blue by the indirect lighting that illuminated the space. "Roark Black. You have a very curvy…" His attention shifted and the next thing Elizabeth knew, she was drowning in his penetrating gaze. "Head line."

"A what?" Her dry mouth prevented anything more from emerging.

"Head line." His fingertip retraced its invigorating journey across her palm. "See here. A curvy head line means you like to play with new ideas. Do you, Elizabeth?"

"Do I what?" The air in the loft had grown thin in the last sixty seconds. Light-headed, she was having trouble getting enough oxygen.

"Do you like playing with new ideas?"

Bad boy. Bad boy.

Elizabeth cleared her throat and retrieved her hand in a short jerk that made Roark's crooked smile widen and heat rush to her face.

"I like creating unique party spaces, if that's what you mean."

It wasn't. His smirk told her so.

"I like what you've done with the place."

More comfortable talking about her job than herself, Elizabeth crossed her arms over her chest and surveyed all she'd accomplished in the past twenty-four hours.

"There wasn't much to it when I got started. Just a concrete floor and white walls. And those incredible arched windows with that spectacular view." She pointed out the latter, hoping to steer his unnerving stare away from her.

"I heard you came up with the idea of a slide show to honor Tyler."

Tyler Banks had died the year before. A thoroughly disliked

human being, no one had any idea that he'd been behind twenty percent of all major New York City charitable donations in the past decade.

"While he was alive, he might not have wanted anyone to know all the wonderful things he'd done, but so many people were helped by his generosity. I thought he deserved a proper tribute."

"Beautiful and smart." His eyes devoured her. "Okay, I'm hooked."

And so was she. Naturally. Bad boys were the bane of her romantic existence. The worse they were, the more she wanted them.

From everything she'd heard and read about Roark Black, she'd expected him to be an arrogant, unprincipled jerk. Gorgeous and sexy, to be sure, but with questionable ethics. The sort of guy she'd have tumbled head over high heels for a year ago.

But after what had happened with Colton last October, she'd sworn on her sister's grave that she was done with all bad boys.

Unfortunately, since those seemed to be the only sort that tripped her trigger, her love life had been in sad shape these past twelve months. Which explained why her hormones had jerked to attention the instant Roark strolled into the party.

"I suggest you get unhooked, Mr. Black," she said, hoping her tart voice would counteract her sweet, gooey insides. Honestly, it was embarrassing to let a man, even a sexy, gorgeous one, turn her into a marshmallow.

"You don't like me?" He didn't appear particularly concerned that she didn't. In fact, he seemed as if he might just relish the challenge.

"I don't know you."

"But you've formed an opinion. How is that fair?"

Fair? He wanted to play fair? She didn't believe that for a second. In fact, she suspected if she gave him the slightest encouragement, she'd find herself in a bathroom with her hem above her ears.

To her dismay a tingle erupted between her thighs. Annoyance added more heat to her next statement than she intended. "I've read things."

"What sort of things?"

He was the reason this party was happening. If he hadn't talked Tyler's granddaughter into letting Waverly's auction off the rarest of Tyler's vast wine collection, there would have been no reason for this event and she would not have been selected as the planner.

All at once she wished she'd just kept her mouth shut. The man was too confident. His personality too strong. And she'd overstepped her role as event planner the second she'd let him engage her. "Things."

Bold, dark eyebrows twitched above keen green-gray eyes. "Oh, don't get all coy with me after throwing down the gauntlet."

No one had ever accused her of being coy before. "Look, it's none of my business, and I really need to make sure everything is all right with the party."

He moved to block her path. "Not before you answer my question."

At six feet three inches, he was a big barrier as he crowded her against the concrete pillar that had hidden their encounter from the prying eyes of the rest of the guests. To Elizabeth's dismay, her body reacted positively to his intimidating size. Lightning flashed in her midsection and zinged along her nerves, leaving a disquieting buzz in its wake.

"You have an opinion." He placed a hand on the column above her shoulder. "I'd like to hear it."

"I don't understand why."

From what she'd heard about him, he didn't really care what anyone thought. Or said. He did his thing and to hell with the rules or what was proper. And to the detriment of her anti-bad-boy pledge, his absolute confidence excited her.

"Let's just say you're the first woman in a long time that's not just playing hard to get. I believe you mean it." He leaned closer. "I'd like to know why."

Rattled by the way his nearness affected her heart rate, she blurt out, "Waverly's is in trouble. If it goes down, you could be the biggest reason why." Mortified by what she'd just said, Elizabeth held her breath and waited for the fallout.

"And where did you read that?" He looked neither surprised nor annoyed with her blunt proclamation.

"I'm sorry," she muttered. "It's none of my business. I should be getting back to the party."

"Not so fast." He surveyed her through narrowed eyes. His charm had vanished. Mouth tight, every tense muscle promising dire consequences if she denied him, he said, "I think you owe me an explanation."

"I spoke out of turn."

"But with a fair amount of knowledge." The dashing man of adventure had given way to a flint-eyed hunter.

Elizabeth quivered, but not in fear. The reckless part of her she'd worked so hard to refine responded to Roark's dangerous vibe. "Look—"

Before she had to explain herself, she was saved by the appearance of Kendra Darling, Elizabeth's old school friend and assistant to Ann Richardson, CEO of Waverly's.

"Mr. Black, Ann sent me to find you."

"Can it wait? Elizabeth and I were having a little chat."

Behind her tortoise-shell glasses, Kendra's large hazel eyes widened as she recognized whom Roark had cornered with his charismatic presence. "It's important," she said. "Some men showed up to talk to you." Kendra's slim body practically quivered with anxiety as she clasped her hands at her waist. "They're with the FBI."

Teeth clenched in irritation, Roark pushed away from Elizabeth and nodded to Ann's flustered assistant. "Tell her I'll be there in a couple of minutes."

"I think she'd like you to come right now."

In other words, the assistant didn't want to return without him. She was used to dealing with wealthy, sometimes difficult clients, not law enforcement. Otherwise she'd know that the FBI liked to chat with him whenever something questionable happened with Middle Eastern antiquities. He'd been both the subject of inquiries and the expert that helped them take down the thieves.

Before heading back to the party, Roark gave Elizabeth one last look. The stunning blonde hadn't moved during his brief exchange with Ann's assistant. In fact, she looked as if she'd like to melt right into the concrete support behind her.

He considered how many times he'd held a relic in his hands and immediately known whether the artifact was genuine or an excellent forgery. His gut had never been wrong, and he'd backed up every authentication with careful, detailed analysis.

This encounter with Elizabeth had hit him the same way. He'd held her hand in his and recognized she was the genuine article. No artifice. No games. Pure attraction. And he intended to have her.

"We'll continue this conversation later," he assured her.

Her eyes said: *don't count on it.*

"Mr. Black?"

He strode away from the petite event planner with the lush figure and unforgettable indigo eyes and made a beeline toward the two obvious outsiders bracketing Ann. Unlike her assistant, Waverly's CEO wasn't in the least bit flustered that FBI agents had crashed the party. Her calm under pressure was one of the things Roark liked most about the head of Waverly's.

Her gaze locked on him as he neared. Eyes hard, she offered him a neutral smile. "Roark, these are Special Agents Matthews and Todd. They would like to ask us a few questions in private."

Roark eyed each in turn, recognizing Todd as an agent he'd seen in passing, but had never had any direct interaction with. Agent Matthews was brand-new. Tall and lean with black hair that spilled over her shoulders in abundant waves. Her dark brown eyes had tracked his progress across the room toward them, and Roark knew this one looked at him and thought career advancement.

"We can speak out on the terrace." Whipping off his tuxedo jacket, he draped it over Ann's shoulders as they headed to the door that led out onto a small outdoor space. Elizabeth's deft touch could be seen here, as well. With white lights tangled in white pine boughs and candles in modern hurricane lanterns, the terrace oozed romance.

After three months in the jungle, Roark appreciated the cool November evening as he enjoyed the glow of Manhattan visible beyond the terrace's cement half wall. Most of the time he found the city too tame for his taste. But there was no denying it sparkled at night.

As soon as the door shut behind them, Roark spoke.

"What can we help you with?"

"This is about Rayas's missing Gold Heart statue," the first FBI agent said. "We've had a new report from Prince Mallik Khouri that a masked man with Mr. Black's exact build stole the statue from his rooms at the royal palace."

"You can't possibly think Roark stole the statue," Ann protested, but it was all for show. She didn't look a bit surprised that Roark was being accused of theft.

"We have reports that he was in Dubai at the time," said Agent Matthews. "It wouldn't be impossible for a man of his talents…" the FBI agent twisted the last word to indicate what she thought of Roark's abilities "…to slip into Rayas, get into the palace and steal the statue."

"It's completely within my power to do so."

Ann's grim glance told him to let her handle the accusation. "He wouldn't."

"Just like a thousand other illegal things are in my power to do," Roark continued, staring Agent Matthews down. "But I don't do them."

"Sorry if we can't take your word for it," Special Agent Todd said.

"There's no proof that Roark was involved." Ann showed no sign of believing otherwise and Roark appreciated that whatever her opinion of him, she hadn't thrown him to the wolves.

"The thief made the mistake of cursing during the scuffle." Matthews nodded. "The voice was deep and very distinctive." Her gaze locked on Roark. "He claims it was your voice, Mr. Black."

"We met briefly once in Dubai years ago. I can't imagine that he'd remember my voice."

But Roark recognized that he was the perfect scapegoat. And Mallik had another reason to suspect that Roark would break into his rooms at the palace.

"Why is this the first we're hearing about this thief?" Roark demanded.

"Prince Mallik was embarrassed to explain his failure to stop the thief to his nephew, the crown prince." Matthews arched her brows. "But he's convinced it was you."

"He's mistaken," Roark snapped.

Ann put her hand on his arm and spoke in a calm, but firm voice. "I've met Prince Mallik. He seemed like an honest, gracious person. However, in the midst of a fight, I imagine being overwhelmed by adrenaline, with heightened senses, he may only think he heard Roark's voice. Didn't you say the thief wore a mask?" Ann didn't wait for the FBI to confirm her statement. "Perhaps his voice was distorted by the cloth."

Roark was working hard to keep his temper at a low simmer. "Have you questioned Dalton Rothschild about the theft?" The rival auction house owner had been a thorn in Waverly's side for years. "He's got a bone to pick with Waverly's and I wouldn't put it past him to send one of his minions to Rayas to steal the statue and pin the blame on me."

"Dalton Rothschild doesn't share your controversial methods for procuring artifacts, Mr. Black," Agent Matthews said. "We would have no reason to question him in this matter."

Of course they wouldn't. It wouldn't surprise Roark to find out that Rothschild was the one that pointed the FBI to Waverly's in the first place. The guy was a slick operator, but as greedy as they came.

While Ann escorted the FBI out, Roark stayed on the terrace and let the chilly fall air cool his ire. Through the large half-circle windows he searched the party for Elizabeth Minerva. She drifted through the well-dressed guests like a wraith, her blond hair confined in a neat French twist, stunning figure downplayed by the simple, long-sleeved black dress.

Hot anger became sizzling desire in seconds. From the moment he'd set eyes on her an hour ago, he'd been preoccupied. Petite, curvaceous blondes weren't really his type. He preferred his women long and lean with flashing black eyes and golden skin. Passion ruled him when it came to antiquities and lovemaking.

His sexual appetites would probably break a dainty, graceful creature like Elizabeth.

"Roark, what are you staring at?"

Without his notice, Ann had returned to the terrace and stood beside him. Roark cursed his preoccupation. Being caught unaware could get him killed in many of the places he ventured.

"How can I get in touch with your party planner?" he asked.

"My assistant made all the arrangements." She sounded surprised that he'd asked. "I'll have her email you the contact information."

"Wonderful. In a few weeks we're going to have reason to celebrate."

"You mean because of the Gold Heart statue?" Ann paced toward the terrace wall. "Are you sure it's not the one stolen from Rayas?"

"Are you asking me if I stole it?" He'd grown weary of her lack of trust in him these past few years.

"Of course not," she said, her tone smooth and unhurried. "But you're sure your source for the statue is completely legitimate?"

"Absolutely." He touched her arm. "You can trust me."

Some of the tension seeped out of her. "I know, but with this new accusation, we have to be more careful than ever."

And careful wasn't something he was known for.

"I need you to bring me the statue," she continued. "The quickest way to resolve this issue is for me to take the statue to Rayas and have the sheikh verify that it isn't the one stolen from the palace."

"It's not."

"Neither the FBI nor Crown Prince Raif Khouri are going to take your word for it." A determined firmness came over Ann's expression. "You've been missing for three months, Roark. Waverly's is in trouble."

He might have been off the grid, but that didn't mean he was out of the loop. Roark knew about the collusion scandal that had rocked Waverly's and Ann Richardson's link to it. His half brother, Vance Waverly, was convinced the CEO had never been romantically involved with Dalton Rothschild and that there was no truth to the rumor of price fixing between the rival auction houses. Roark trusted Vance's faith in Ann where illegal practices were concerned, but he wasn't as convinced that Rothschild's hostile takeover of Waverly's was just hearsay. Nor was he sure Ann hadn't fallen for Dalton. Which meant Roark wasn't sure how far he could trust Ann.

"It's important to clear up the matter of the statue," Ann continued, handing him back his tuxedo jacket.

"I understand, but getting the statue here quickly is going to present a problem."

"What do you mean?"

"I mean with all the publicity surrounding the statue and Rothschild's obvious determination to cause a problem with the auction, it's more important than ever to safeguard it."

"Get it here as fast as you can. Or it may be too late to save Waverly's."

Ann Richardson's resolve resonated with Roark. He faced difficult situations with the same strength of purpose. It was part of the reason why he was willing to do what it took to help her save Waverly's.

In a thoughtful mood, he escorted her inside. While Roark slipped back into the jacket, he noticed a pair of eyes on him. They belonged to a very influential member of Waverly's board. Something behind the man's stare piqued Roark's curiosity. He snagged a glass of champagne from a passing waitress and strode over to shake the man's hand.

"Nice collection you secured," George Cromwell said. "I had no idea Tyler was such a connoisseur."

"He was a man of many secrets."

Cromwell lifted his glass. "Here's to hoping he takes most of them to the grave."

Roark offered a polite smile while impatience churned in his gut. Was he seeing trouble where there was none? Had his instincts been wrong about what he'd glimpsed in the man's manner? Or was he growing paranoid after years of dodging danger and the past three months spent in a deadly game of hide and seek with a bloodthirsty cartel?

"What were the FBI doing here tonight?" Cromwell asked.

Reassured that his instincts were right on track, Roark offered the board member a dismissive smile. "They'd received some bad information and came to clear up the matter." In its own way, this concrete jungle was just as perilous as the tropical one he'd left behind.

"And was it cleared up?"

Roark wasn't going to lie. "I believe they still have some doubts."

Cromwell grew grim. "I'm concerned about Waverly's future."

"How so?" Roark sipped at his champagne and played at nonchalance. He hated all the political maneuvering and missed the familiar danger inherent in guns, knives and criminals who didn't hesitate to kill anyone who got in their way.

"A number of Waverly's shareholders have been approached about selling our shares."

"Let me guess," Roark said, annoyance flaring. "Rothschild?"

"Yes."

"Selling to him wouldn't be in anyone's best interest."

"With the troubles of late, there is concern that Waverly's is being mismanaged." Cromwell was both stating his opinion and digging for information.

Roark's true connection to Vance Waverly wasn't mainstream knowledge, but a few people knew Vance and Roark shared a father. If Cromwell assumed Roark would divulge what he knew about Waverly's problems, he'd be wrong.

"That's ridiculous. Ann is the perfect choice to run Waverly's. Any troubles we've had recently can be attributed to one person. Dalton Rothschild."

"Perhaps. But your activities of late haven't helped."

Roark remained silent. It would do no good to protest that what he did had no bearing on Waverly's, but as long as he remained connected to the auction house, anything he brought in would be suspect. Being someone accustomed to operating alone, Roark found a sense of discomfort stirring in him to have others relying on him.

"What I do is completely legal and legitimate."

"Of course." The board member nodded. "But the world of business is not always interested in facts. Markets rise and fall on people's perceptions of what's going on."

"And I'm being perceived as…?"

"Too freewheeling in both your professional and personal lives."

Roark couldn't argue. He based his actions on his needs and desires. Taking others into consideration wasn't part of the equation. But the older man's assessment poked at a tender spot, bruised earlier by the scathing opinion of a petite blonde.

His attention wandered in her direction. He knew exactly where she was. Her presence was a shaft of light to his senses.

Pleasure flashed like lightning along his nerve endings when he caught her staring at him. He winked at her and grinned as she turned away so fast she almost plowed into a passing server.

Oblivious to Roark's momentary distraction, the board member continued, "I think if you could demonstrate that you're committed to Waverly's, I could convince the other board members that you, Vance and Ann are the future we want."

"And how would you suggest I do that?"

"Show us and the world that you've settled down."

In other words, postpone any dangerous operations for the near future. That could be problematic. Roark was now in pursuit of a new rare artifact—the second half of a pair of leopard heads that had once graced the throne of Tipu Sultan, an important figure in Indian and Islamic history. The first head, encrusted with diamonds, emeralds and rubies, had been discovered in a long-forgotten trunk in Winnipeg, Canada, and auctioned several years earlier.

The buyer was a collector of Middle Eastern art and had offered Roark access to the one-of-a-kind documents in his private library if Roark could find the second leopard. The knowledge locked up in the collector's home was worth way more to Roark than the half million dollars that the man had originally offered as a finder's fee.

Roark's gaze swept the party guests until he located Ann Richardson. "I'd planned to leave New York in the next few days."

"That's not a good idea if you're at all concerned about the future of Waverly's."

Roark tensed as the jaws of responsibility clamped down on him. "I have business in Dubai."

"Do you think that leaving town is a good idea while the FBI is interested in you?" George Cromwell nodded sagely at Roark's scowl. "Stay in New York. Demonstrate that your personal life has stabilized."

"Stabilized how?"

"Your romantic exploits are legendary. If you could settle down with one woman, that would convince everyone you're the man we need at the helm."

Roark ignored the sensation of a noose being tossed over his head and kept his body relaxed. Settle down with the love of his life. Not so easy for a man whose one true passion involved dangerous, globe-hopping adventures. No woman, no matter how lush, blonde and adorable, could compete with the thrill of discovering what had been lost for centuries.

But the prospects of Waverly's depended on his ability to project a stable, reliable image. What he needed was a woman who could play the part of his adoring girlfriend. Someone who understood this was for the good of Waverly's.

That way, when it ended, he wouldn't need to worry about breaking her heart.

Roark grinned. "It's funny you should bring this up now because I've been seeing someone for a while and we're very close to taking our relationship public."

"Wonderful." The board member covered his surprise with a relieved smile. "Bring her around for dinner tomorrow night and we'll discuss your future in more detail."

"We'll be there."

"Looking forward to it. What's your lady's name?"

"Elizabeth." Roark glanced toward the screened-off section of the loft. If he had to be settled down by a woman, he intended to choose one who intrigued him. "Elizabeth Minerva."

Two

Elizabeth barely noticed the exuberant buzz filling the offices of Josie Summers's Event Planning as she navigated the halls. A large coffee clutched in her hand, she thanked the coworkers who congratulated her on the success of the previous night's wine auction. Normally, the well wishes perked her up. She'd worked hard to become Josie's top earner and enjoyed the prestige it brought her.

Success had come easily since she had started immersing herself in her work a year ago, to keep despair at bay after her sister's death. If she was busy, she had no time to fall prey to the depression that lurked in the shadows. It wasn't long before she discovered that running herself into a state of exhaustion wasn't something she could do forever.

She needed a personal life, but thanks to her rotten taste in men, dating brought her more heartache than happiness.

What had struck her hard after losing her sister, brother-in-law and niece in a car accident was how alone she was. Her parents had moved from upstate New York to Oregon right as Elizabeth started her freshman year of college. In the seven years they'd been gone, they'd never returned to the East coast. It was as if with both their children grown, they'd started this whole new life for themselves.

When they'd first announced that they were moving Elizabeth had been bothered by their abandonment. But after she moved to New York City and started college, she'd fallen in love. Not with a man, but with the city. The excitement and the possibilities of living in such a wonderful place. And she'd never once felt lonely.

It had helped that her sister was a couple hours away by train. But with Stephanie's death, a hole had appeared in her heart. What she wanted was a family. That's when she decided to make a family of her own. Unfortunately, as fabulously as her career was progressing, things on the baby front weren't going so well. Two rounds of in vitro had failed.

She was all out of money. Her dreams of motherhood wouldn't be coming true this year.

Elizabeth's heart wrenched in dismay.

She should be flying high. Last night's triumph was yet another step upward professionally. She was crossing career goals off her list ahead of schedule. But what good did all her success do her when the reason she was working so hard was to provide for the child her body refused to conceive?

Maybe if she'd been more positive during the second in vitro try. Kept her hopes up. Spent her days and nights visualizing a baby in her arms rather than bracing herself for disappointment. Maybe then things would have turned out better.

If her sister could hear her thoughts, she'd agree. Stephanie had been an advocate for positive thinking since she was a freshman in high school. Top of her class. Head cheerleader. Captain of the women's volleyball team the year they won state. Whatever Stephanie visualized, she made happen.

And what would her sister say about Elizabeth's pity party for one? Stephanie would tell her to pull out a piece of paper and write her goal at the top, then list all the things she could do to move forward.

Elizabeth settled her purse in a drawer and hung up her coat.

Flopping into her desk chair, she set a yellow legal pad in front of her and wrote *Motherhood* at the top. Below that she doodled dollar signs.

How to afford more in vitro treatments? Save money until she could afford to try again. Economizing wasn't the answer. She already lived in the smallest apartment she could stand, a tiny studio in Chelsea with a view of the neighboring building's wall. What she needed to do was increase her income. And the fastest way to do that? Demand that Josie make her a partner. She was already bringing in more money than all of Josie's other planners combined. It was time she reaped some of the benefits of all her hard work.

Feeling more determined than when she'd left her apartment an hour ago, Elizabeth headed for her boss's office. With each step she took, she gained confidence in her plan.

It was the perfect opportunity to make her pitch. Last night's party had been a huge success. She'd made a dozen contacts and fielded interest from at least eight people who wanted her to help with their holiday parties. Her career was about to go from fast track to supersonic.

"Josie, do you have a second?"

The fifty-eight-year-old head of Josie Summers's Event Planning sat like a queen on a cream damask sofa in her enormous corner office. A silver tray with an elegant coffeepot sat on the low table before her. On the round table that stood halfway between the door and her boss's ornate cherry desk was a vase overflowing with the most gorgeous long-stemmed red roses Elizabeth had ever seen. Things must be going better between Josie and her boyfriend of twelve years.

Her boss waved Elizabeth in. "Darling, we're a triumph."

"Everyone seemed to enjoy themselves," Elizabeth said. "The auction raised three million for children's cancer research." She sat beside Josie and accepted the cup of coffee her boss handed her. "Kendra called me this morning and said her boss was pleased with our handling of the event."

Even though Josie hadn't been involved with any aspect of the planning, she claimed credit for every success.

"Well, I should say so." Josie crossed her legs and leaned forward to pour coffee into a second china cup. She sipped and eyed Elizabeth over the rim. "Josie Summers's Event Planning offers nothing but sublime perfection."

"Absolutely." Having her boss take credit for her successes didn't sit well with Elizabeth, but she needed her job and wanted to keep it.

Until coming to work for Josie, she'd never been one to tout her accomplishments. She'd always done her best without expecting anyone to praise her. But it hadn't taken more than six months in the cutthroat world of event planning for her to realize that if she wanted to get ahead, she not only needed to be the best, she had to make sure everyone knew it.

"I've already received a half dozen calls this morning about upcoming events thanks to the work we did last night." The diamonds in Josie's ears winked. "Josie Summers's Event Planning is the best in New York. It's about time everyone recognized that."

Thanks to all Elizabeth's hard work. She forced a smile. "That's great. And part of what I wanted to talk to you about this morning…"

"Oh, and those came for you." Josie indicated the roses. "They were delivered to me by mistake."

Elizabeth regarded the extravagant bouquet. She felt oddly light-headed. It was the sort of thing a man sent the woman he loved. "For me?"

Josie picked up a small white card and handed it to Elizabeth. "Another admirer, from the looks of it."

Stifling her resentment that her boss had already read the card, Elizabeth slid it out of the envelope and stared at the bold script.

I have a proposal I'd like to discuss with you. RB

She had no trouble imagining the sort of *proposal* Roark Black had in mind. Proposition was more like it. Remembering the way his gaze had slipped over her last night, heat rushed into her cheeks. Conscious of her boss's avid curiosity, she mastered her expression and held very still. Difficult when she wanted to run from the room and the implications of that message. But fleeing would do her no good when the danger lay inside her. The searing curiosity about the enigmatic treasure hunter. What would it be like to have those mobile lips capture hers? His hands gliding over her skin as if she was a priceless artifact he'd been searching for all his life?

"Elizabeth?"

"Hmm?"

Josie's voice held amusement. "Who is RB?"

She dug her nails into her palm to disperse the sensual fog that she'd gotten lost in. Lying would do her no good. Josie's curiosity was fully engaged. She would dig until she was satisfied she knew everything that was going on with Elizabeth.

"Roark Black."

"Really?" Interest flared in Josie's brown eyes. "I didn't realize you knew him."

"He was at the wine auction last night." Elizabeth could see her boss jump to the wrong conclusion. "He was impressed with the work I'd done for the party. Perhaps he wants to hire me."

"This is a first," Josie purred, her opinion about the true reason for the bouquet already formed. "I've never seen two dozen red roses accompany a job offer before."

"Mr. Black is a unique individual."

"With unique tastes, I imagine."

Elizabeth responded with a tight smile. "I'd better go give him a call." She stood, eager to escape her boss's keen gaze. She was halfway to the door when Josie stopped her.

"Don't forget your roses."

"Silly me," Elizabeth said, her teeth gritted together.

"And let me know what he has in mind. This is the opening I've been waiting for. A chance to move Josie Summers's Event Planning into a whole new level. Event planner to the rich and famous."

"Thanks to me," Elizabeth muttered into the sumptuous roses.

It wasn't until she returned to her office that she realized Roark Black's *proposal* had distracted her from her plan to ask Josie about making her a partner. How much longer was she going to build Josie's business without getting the rewards she deserved?

Setting the roses on her desk, Elizabeth perched on one of her guest chairs and dialed the number on the back of Roark's card.

"Hello, Elizabeth."

His deep voice, rich with amusement, sent a tingle up her spine. With two words he'd sparked a chain reaction inside her. She flopped back in the chair and closed her eyes to better concentrate on his seductive voice.

"Hello, Mr. Black," she responded, her tone less professional than she wanted. "Thank you for the roses."

"Roark," he corrected, his tone somewhere between a command and a request. "I'm glad you like them."

She hadn't said that. "They're beautiful."

"Beautiful roses for a beautiful lady."

His smooth compliments were having a detrimental effect on her professionalism. Flutters attacked her stomach. Warmth flooded her as delight scampered along her nerve endings. Her body appeared to have a mind of its own, wanting to curl up in the chair and cradle the phone like some smitten teenager.

"The card mentioned you had a job for me?"

"A proposal," he corrected, caressing the word.

"What sort of proposal?"

"I'd like to discuss it in person."

And she'd prefer to arrange everything over the phone so his enticing sex appeal wouldn't prove her undoing. "Would you like to come to my office this afternoon?"

"I was thinking perhaps you could meet me at my apartment. Say in an hour?"

"Your apartment..." She trailed off, at a loss for words since she didn't dare accuse him of hitting on her when she wasn't completely sure what was going on.

"Don't you visit a client's apartment when you're planning a party for them?"

"You want me to plan a party?" Her relief came through loud and clear.

"Of course." He sounded amused. "What did you think I wanted?"

The arrogance of the man.

Elizabeth fumed for about five seconds and then reminded herself that this was business and she was a businesswoman. She'd worked with demanding clients before. Just because Roark Black was sinfully handsome and dangerously exciting was no reason to let her baser instincts get the better of her. He was a client. Nothing more.

"An hour and a half," she countered, feeling ridiculous the second the words were out of her mouth. It was silly to try to play power games with this man when all he had to do was hit her with his crooked grin and every sensible thought fled her mind.

"I'll text you my address."

At one minute to ten, she stood outside Roark's loft in Soho. She recognized her nerves had gotten the better of her when she'd gone home to change into a sweater dress in a silvery blue. She loved the color. It intensified the gold tones of her hair and drew out the flecks of cobalt in her eyes. But most important, the outfit gave her confidence.

Briefcase clutched before her, weight on the balls of her feet, she awaited the appearance of the first man in a year who'd imperiled her no-bad-boys edict. Pulse hammering, she dredged up every hurt and disappointment caused by the men she'd chosen over the years. Remembering past injuries took the edge off her unwelcome excitement at seeing Roark again.

And then, the door opened, revealing him in all his male splendor. He was dressed casually in worn denim and a long-sleeved gray shirt that intensified the smoky tones in his eyes.

"Elizabeth." Her name sighed out of him like a lover's exhalation. "You are even more beautiful than I remembered."

Crap. Her heart fluttered like some idiotic debutant at her first cotillion.

"And you are more charming than ever." Her voice snapped like a whip, snatching the compliment right out of the words.

He grinned at her, unfazed by her tartness. "Come in."

The loft was as incredible as she'd expected. Sixteen-foot

ceilings, enormous arched windows, exposed brick everywhere she looked. Wood floors gleamed beneath couches slip-covered in white. The living space was so huge he was able to have three separate sitting areas. One flanked the stone fireplace at the far end. One clustered in front of the floor-to-ceiling bookshelves near an opening that she guessed led to the bedrooms. A third near the open kitchen with its dark granite countertops and stainless-steel appliances.

"This is nice," Elizabeth murmured, reflecting on the shoe-box she lived in. "Perfect for entertaining. How many people are you inviting?"

"I was thinking about a hundred or so."

Elizabeth pulled out an electronic tablet and began jotting notes. "Did you have a date picked out?"

"I was thinking next Saturday."

"That is short notice."

Mentally running through her bookings, she keyed up her schedule, already knowing she had the Hendersons' tenth wedding anniversary on that evening. The arrangements were all made. It was the sort of party Brenda could handle on her own.

"I'm happy to compensate you for any inconvenience it might cause."

Elizabeth offered him a bright smile as she mentally calculated her commission. "What sort of party did you have in mind?"

"It's an engagement party."

"How nice." And how surprising. She'd never pictured Roark Black hosting something like that. The man had commitment issues written all over him. "Who's the lucky couple?"

"We are."

Incomprehension fogged her indigo-blue eyes as she looked up at him. "We are what?"

"The happy engaged couple I'm throwing the party for."

Her crisp professionalism wrinkled beneath the weight of her confusion. "We're not engaged."

"Not yet."

The expression in her eyes went from shell-shocked to resolute. "Not ever."

"I'm crushed." He shouldn't enjoy teasing her so much, but it seemed the only way to get past her guards and reach the woman behind the event planner.

"I doubt it." She'd recovered her equilibrium and now regarded him with open skepticism. "Perhaps you should explain what's going on."

"Last night you jumped all over me about how I was going to be the downfall of Waverly's."

"I merely suggested you might be a contributing factor."

"You weren't the only one thinking that way."

Her eyes narrowed. "Not surprising. But what does that have to do with why I'm here?"

"A certain member of the Waverly's board mentioned that he's been approached by Dalton Rothschild about selling his shares and has been asked to persuade others on the board to follow suit. He doesn't want Rothschild to take over Waverly's, but needs a good reason to continue to support the current leadership at Waverly's."

She nodded, but remained silent while her steady gaze encouraged him to proceed.

"He thinks that leadership needs to include me, but recent events have raised questions about my activities. He indicated if I could demonstrate that I'm leaving behind my proclivity for trouble, the board would feel more confident about the stability of Waverly's."

"And you think an engagement will make you more respectable."

"It was suggested a stable personal life would inspire confidence in my upstanding behavior."

"Why me?"

While his address book was bursting with women who would jump at the chance to play his fiancée, Elizabeth was unaffected by his money or his charm. She intrigued him.

"After last night's passionate denouncement of me and your

concern for the future of Waverly's, I thought you would be the perfect choice for a pretend engagement."

His last two words caused a profound reaction. Her muscles relaxed and she almost smiled. "Find someone else."

"I've already decided on you."

"Surely there are more suitable women in the circles you frequent that would be happy to perpetrate this ruse with you."

"None more suitable than you." And he meant it.

The concern she'd shown for Waverly's had inspired him to make her his co-conspirator in his scheme to improve his image. And the active dislike she was struggling so hard to maintain intrigued him. Winning her over presented an enchanting challenge. And if he was going to be stuck in New York for the uncertain future, he would need something exciting to occupy himself. Elizabeth Minerva fit the bill.

"Does it strike you at all counterproductive that you're trying to inspire confidence in your upstanding behavior by presenting a fake fiancée to your friends and family?"

"See, this is why I need you. Not one other woman I know dives straight to the heart of my shortcomings the way you do."

Her full lips twitched. "And somehow you perceive this as a good thing?"

Despite her skepticism, Elizabeth hadn't slammed the door on his proposition. Or at least, she hadn't stormed out of his loft and put an end to the conversation. If he could keep her around for a few more minutes, he knew he could convince her how much he needed her help.

"Last night you were right. Waverly's is in trouble. Dalton Rothschild is after the board members to sell. I'm in a perfect position to stop him." He hit her with all the seriousness in his arsenal. "And you are in a perfect position to help me do so. Think of what will happen to all the employees who've been with Waverly's for years. If Rothschild takes over, what do you think he's going to do with them?"

"You aren't playing fair." Her gaze skidded away from his.

At that moment, he knew he had her. "We'll make this a business arrangement. Consider it a contract job. Six months and you're free of me. In the meantime, think of all the contacts you'll make as my fiancée. Manhattan's elite will be vying to have you as their event planner."

"A business arrangement," she echoed, eyes narrowing as she searched his expression. "Nothing more?"

"Well, of course there will be public appearances and equally public displays of affection."

She chewed on her lower lip, attention fixed on the far side of the room where floating shelves housed some of the less valuable artifacts he'd brought back from around the world.

"But just public displays of affection. Don't expect to reap any benefits of our engagement in private."

Keeping her in the dark about all his intentions was completely necessary if he hoped to secure her agreement. There would be plenty of time later to demonstrate all the ways their arrangement could be mutually beneficial.

"I promise not to do anything you don't want me to."

Her brows came together. "That didn't answer my question."

"I assure you, anytime I'm involved in a relationship it's the women who have expectations, not me."

"No wonder people find you untrustworthy." Elizabeth shook her head. "You couldn't give a straight answer if your life depended on it."

"And I assure you, from time to time, it has."

"Let me be blunt. I'm not going to sleep with you."

"Who said anything about sleeping." He knew he should stop teasing her, but she was so damned adorable when she got riled up.

"If you think I'm some sort of weak-minded bimbo who will tumble into your bed at the first snap of your fingers, you've picked the wrong girl."

"Easy, sweetheart, I think you're no such thing. I fully expect you to resist me at every turn."

With her blue eyes snapping in ire, color flooding her cheeks and her soft lips parted to deliver scathing retorts, it took all his significant willpower not to draw her into his arms and take advantage of that simmering passion.

His facial muscles twitched as smiling became irresistible. "In fact, I'm counting on it."

Most single New York women would be flattered that Roark Black had chosen them to play the part of his fiancée. Elizabeth suspected a whistle launched from his loft window would bring a dozen or so running. They'd scoff at her reluctance to get cozy with a handsome, eligible bachelor of Roark's financial and social standing even as they trampled her in their rush to vie for his attention.

Was she crazy to hesitate?

There'd been an intense light in his eye as he said he expected her to resist him at every turn that told her she was smart to be wary. Her heart hadn't stopped its distressed thumping the entire distance to Chinatown where her best friend lived. Allison and Elizabeth had been roommates freshman year and had bonded over their pathological need for organization and their mutual dislike of the girl across the hall, Honey Willingham.

"Elizabeth." The leggy woman with dark blond hair and dark circles under her eyes looked at her with delight. "Your timing is perfect. I just got Prince Gregory down for his nap."

"Sorry to stop by without calling." Since Allison had given birth five months ago, Elizabeth hadn't seen her friend more than once a month. To Elizabeth's shame, it stung that Allison was so happy being a mom when Elizabeth struggled to conceive.

"No. It's fine. I'm happy to take any time you can spare."

Her friend didn't mean anything by the remark, but Elizabeth flinched anyway. "I'm a terrible friend."

"No. You're just busy."

So was Allison. She had her hands full with a colicky baby, but she managed to call three times a week. Elizabeth felt even worse.

"How's Greg?"

"Getting better." Allison led Elizabeth into the tiny kitchen and fetched a couple diet sodas out of the refrigerator. "He sleeps almost four hours a night now."

"Yikes."

Elizabeth tried to imagine how she was going to make things work on her own with a baby and no help. She glanced around the kitchen. Dishes were piled in the sink and baby bottles sat upside down in a drying rack. Beyond the breakfast bar, where once there had been a pristine living room with glass tables, expensive accent pieces and tons of plants, only the black leather couch remained and it was piled with a basket of unfolded baby clothes. Colorful toys and a baby swing competed for space on the hardwood floors.

"Can I babysit for you and Keith one night? Maybe you could go out for a nice dinner?"

Allison looked so hopeful, Elizabeth's heart clenched.

"That would be great. Get you ready for your own bundle of joy." This last was said with such weariness that Elizabeth wondered if her envy over her friend's perfect life had been a tad off base. Gasping, Allison leaned forward and grabbed Elizabeth's hands. Her eyes burned with hope. "Is that why you're here? To tell me you're pregnant?"

"No." Elizabeth shook her head. "The last round didn't take."

"Damn." Allison's mouth turned down at the corners. "I'm so sorry. What are you going to do?"

"Try again."

"But I thought you didn't have enough money."

"I'm going to ask Josie to make me a partner."

Allison blew out a breath. "Good luck with that." She looked immediately contrite. "I'm sorry. That wasn't what you needed to hear. How are you going to approach it?"

In the face of Allison's doubt, Elizabeth pushed aside her frustration and squared her shoulders. "I just handled my first A-list party and it was a huge success. All sorts of bookings are coming in and they all want me."

"How wonderful. Does Josie know they all want you?"

On the topic of Elizabeth's career, Allison had all sorts of strong opinions about Josie Summers. All of them negative.

"In her own way, she knows." But that didn't mean Josie would ever admit it.

"You could quit," Allison suggested with a far too innocent expression. "Start your own event planning company."

"You know I can't do that." It was a conversation she and Allison had engaged in often in the past three years.

"I know you're afraid to do that."

"I like the security of a job with a steady paycheck."

Allison didn't appear convinced by Elizabeth's determined tone. "You could put off having a baby for a couple years while you get your business going."

Elizabeth rejected her friend's suggestion with a firm shake of her head. "I'd rather put up with Josie for the next five years than wait to have a baby."

"You're so sensible." The baby monitor on the counter next to the sink erupted with cries. Allison stared at the device and held her breath as if even that small noise would further disturb the restless child.

"Do you need to go check on him?"

"No. He should settle down." But the cries became more insistent and Allison heaved a weary sigh. "I guess fifteen minutes is going to be all he can handle today. I don't know why he doesn't collapse with exhaustion. I'm tired and he gets less sleep than I do. I'll be right back."

Elizabeth expected to have to finish her conversation with Allison over the wails of the baby, but almost as soon as she vanished into her son's room, the monitor stopped emitting noise. She returned with her son in her arms.

"Can you hold this momma's boy for a second?" Without waiting for Elizabeth to answer, Allison handed her the baby. "I swear he lives to drive me crazy. Just like his father." The last she muttered, the words almost intelligible, but Elizabeth heard.

And grinned.

She buried her nose in the baby's neck and inhaled his scent. This is what she was working toward. Why she'd accept Roark's offer to pretend to be his fiancée. She needed to bring in more clients and strengthen her position as Josie's top producer. Becoming a partner would assure her financial security and she could afford to try in vitro again.

Her phone vibrated, reminding Elizabeth that she had work to do. As much as she wished she could linger for the rest of the afternoon, there were clients to contact and arrangements to oversee. If she was gone too long from the office, Brenda might take it upon herself to organize something and that would be extremely bad.

The sun fell across Elizabeth's shoulders as she made her way to the nearest subway station. Visiting Allison's domestic haven had done her good. The parts of her psyche that had seemed frantic and out of control were calmer. She was thinking clearly instead of freaking out. Before she headed down the stairs to catch her train, she pulled out her cell phone.

Almost as if he'd been expecting her call, Roark picked up before the second ring.

"Okay, Mr. Black, we have a deal."

"Just like that?" Despite his words, he almost purred with satisfaction. "We haven't even discussed what you want in return."

"All I want is the chance to make the sort of connections that will further my career."

"And you'll meet plenty of people who will want to hire you. But I'm going to take up a significant amount of your time and I intend to compensate you for it."

"How much time?"

"To be credible we need to be seen together four hours a night, twice maybe three times a week for six months. Twenty thousand dollars is a nice round number, don't you think?"

She stared at the sky and blinked back a sudden rush of tears. Her relief was so profound, for a moment she couldn't breathe. With that much money she could afford to try in vitro again almost immediately. A twinge of conscience returned her to reality.

"That's too much. I wouldn't feel comfortable."

"The money is for your time, nothing more."

And although every one of her brain cells told her she was crazy, in her heart, she believed him. "It's still too much."

"Very well." A hint of exasperation entered his tone. "What sort of number did you have in mind?"

"Thirteen thousand, four hundred twenty-eight dollars and ninety-seven cents."

A long hesitation followed her words. When he spoke, his voice was rich with laughter. "Are you sure you don't want that rounded up to twenty-nine dollars?"

"No, thank you."

"Care to share what you're going to do with that particular sum?"

She smiled as she imagined the look on his face as she said, "I'm going to use it to get pregnant."

Three

A brisk November wind snatched at Elizabeth's breath as she exited the town car and stared up at the Fifth Avenue apartment building. She shivered in her wool coat. Nine hours ago she'd agreed to Roark's mad scheme, proving once again that whenever she was in the presence of a bad boy, she and common sense took divergent paths.

Roark lifted her hand and brushed warm lips across her chilly fingers. "Have I told you how beautiful you look?"

Several times. "Are you sure everyone is going to believe we're a couple?"

"They will if we seem smitten with each other."

"Smitten." The old-fashioned word struck her as odd coming from someone as masculine as Roark.

"Can you do smitten?"

Given the way her pulse fluttered in giddy delight every time he flashed his wolfish grin, she was pretty sure all she had to do was let nature take its course. "I guess."

"Just follow my lead." He tucked her hand into the crook of his arm and led the way into the building.

The urge to gape at the building's opulent entry almost overpowered her nervousness about the dinner party. It wouldn't do for her to act like some rustic just off the farm. She'd been in New York City since graduating from high school and had planned parties for many wealthy people. But she was about to step up to the big time. Any false move and she would have wasted her chance.

"How exactly are we going to break up?"

Roark shot her a wry glance. "We just started going out and you're already thinking about how things are going to end?"

"A girl has to be practical." So she claimed. Too bad she'd never been able to behave sensibly when it came to her love life.

"Why don't you forget about being practical for a while?"

"Tempting." She offered him a counterfeit smile. "But unrealistic. This is a business deal, remember?"

"I doubt I could forget with you reminding me every ten minutes," he mused. They'd stopped before a door. "Can we discuss the demise of our relationship on the way home?"

"Of course."

A woman in her early forties, wearing a maid's uniform, opened the door for them. Elizabeth stepped through and slipped out of her best winter coat. Because Roark was using her to tone down his reputation as a ladies' man, she wore a conservative wrap dress the color of claret.

With her hair's natural wave flattened by a straight iron and her grandmother's simple garnet drops dangling from her ears, Elizabeth knew she presented a classic, elegant picture.

"Absolutely beautiful," Roark murmured as he placed his hand in the small of her back and escorted her toward the living room where the rest of the guests had gathered.

Their engagement might be a sham, but there was nothing phony about Roark's flattering words or his affectionate tone. The chemistry between them was real. She felt the tug of it every time he took her hand or caressed her with his gaze.

Man, oh man, she was in trouble.

"Good evening, Roark. And this must be the woman who captured your heart. I can understand why. I'm George Cromwell."

Elizabeth recognized the man from the wine auction, but doubted he'd remember her. She worked hard to be a ghost at the events she planned. Always around, but invisible to the guests.

"Elizabeth Minerva," she said. "You have a lovely home."

"My wife has exceptional taste. She picked me after all." He laughed at his own joke. "Let me introduce you."

By the time dinner was announced, Elizabeth had become way too conscious of her tall, handsome companion. He wouldn't stop touching her. Simple brushes of his fingertips at her waist, his palm against the small of her back, his lips across her temple. Grazing contact that demonstrated his adoration for the benefit of all onlookers. If it had been any other man, Elizabeth would have endured it without a blip in her heart rate.

But Roark Black wasn't any other man. He was dangerous, charismatic and intelligent. A lethal combination where her common sense was concerned.

"I just love the way you two can't keep your eyes off each other," murmured Elizabeth's dinner companion. An elegant woman in her mid-fifties, she was on the board of several charities and had promised to call Elizabeth about upcoming events. "Roark is such a favorite of mine. I'm glad he found someone who makes him happy."

Elizabeth smiled to hide her dismay. It was way too easy to act like a woman in love with Roark. Before tonight she'd believed him to be nothing more than a bad boy who charmed women and left a trail of loneliness behind him. But she'd watched him impress everyone with his wit and wry humor and realized there was more to Roark than what the papers printed. Had she taken on more than she could handle?

"That went well," Roark commented as he handed her into the back of his black town car. "I think we managed to convince everyone that you've tamed me."

Her lips twitched. "You're mad if you think anyone believes you tamed."

"Perhaps you're right." Upon entering the car, he'd let his head fall back against the rich leather. Now, he glanced her way, his eyes sparkling. "But they all can see that I've been leashed by the power of my feelings for you."

Despite the fact that his words were completely untrue, Elizabeth couldn't stop the thrill they awakened. Her proclivity for bad boys had its roots in the fantasy that one day she'd meet one she could tame. It was a frustrating dilemma because she wasn't at all attracted to the good guys. They were boring. So what happened if she tamed a bad boy? Would she grow bored?

Elizabeth knew she'd never find out.

"Now can we discuss what happens when those feelings end?"

"You're like a terrier with a rat, aren't you? Pursuing the thing past the point of exhaustion."

She regarded him, unaffected by his mockery. "Something like that."

"Do you want me to be the villain?"

She wasn't completely sure if he was the hero, but he'd been placed in the role of bad guy far too often.

"Since the engagement is supposed to repair your reputation," she said, "that would be counterproductive. Can't we mutually decide it's not going to work?"

"I really think it would be better if you broke my heart." Roark took her hand and placed it on his chest.

Her emotions tumbled as his heart thumped hypnotically against her palm. "And why is that?"

"Because I don't want to ever hurt you."

The tone of the conversation had gone from flirtatious to serious so fast it took her brain a second to catch up.

"That's chivalrous of you." She tugged to free her hand, but not hard enough to break his grip.

His fingertips trailed along her cheek, setting her skin ablaze. "I mean it."

"I know you do," she assured him, pulling his hand from her face. "But you don't need to worry about me. I'll be just fine."

Roark stood in the middle of his living room and marveled. Chased out at eight that morning by the phalanx of workers that had descended on the loft, he'd stayed away until he could no longer bear the curiosity.

In seven hours, Elizabeth had transformed the monochromatic, sterile space into a Moroccan dream. Using the room's height, she'd fashioned a tent of sorts. Gold-shot, jewel-bright fabric, attached to the ceiling and walls, masked the room's industrial feel. She'd removed his white couches and replaced them with chaise lounges. A hundred pillows, all different sizes and colors, covered the plush oriental rugs. Three large punched-metal lamps hung down the center of the room, spilling soft light over the décor.

At the center of all the decadent color and texture stood Elizabeth, classically elegant in a simple navy pantsuit, her hair smoothed into her signature French roll, as she directed last-minute touches of lavish flower arrangements and bowls of apples, dragon fruit, mangos and star fruit.

The urge to ease her down onto a spill of floor pillows and mess up her perfection overtook him. In fact, he took three steps in her direction before he awoke to the realization that they were not alone in his loft. His intention must have been written all over his face because a slim brunette in her mid-thirties stared at him with wide eyes.

"Hello," he said, reeling in his lust. "I'm Roark Black."

"S-Sara Martin. I'm helping Elizabeth with your event."

At the sound of her name, Elizabeth turned and noticed him for the first time. Her serene satisfaction, so dissimilar to the chaotic emotions thundering through his body, increased his craving for her.

"What do you think?" Elizabeth questioned, obviously pleased by the results she'd achieved. "Hard to believe it's a loft in Soho, isn't it?"

The longing to feel a smidgeon of her delight caught him off guard. That whole stop-and-smell-the-roses thing had never been on his agenda. He'd jumped from one adventure to another without pause, almost as if he was running from something. What? Boredom? Loneliness?

What had he gained from his travels except for questions about his character and a bunch of trinkets?

"You've done a wonderful job."

"I hope your friends think so." The tiniest flicker of uncertainty clouded her deep blue eyes.

"They will love it." And her. Conscious of their audience, he stepped into her space and felt her muscles tense. "Relax," he murmured. "Everyone is going to know about us after tonight."

"I know." She lifted her chin and gave him a wobbly smile.

Her soft rosy lips practically demanded his attention, but he kissed her cheek instead, lingering over her fragrant skin, listening to the uneven cadence of her breath. He disturbed her. Good. That was only fair since she made him mad with wanting. He couldn't wait to set her on fire and lose himself in the moist welcome of her body. With effort Roark mastered the urgent craving to sweep her into his arms and mark her as his.

Time enough for that later.

"Can you take a break?"

She nodded. "The caterers should be here any minute, but Sara can supervise their setup."

"Wonderful. Let's go talk in my study. I have something for you."

He guided her into his favorite room in the loft, a cluttered space lined with overflowing bookshelves. It was here that he spent most of his time, surrounded by the ancient texts that helped him unlock secrets to treasures hidden for centuries.

Plucking a black box off a pile of photographs, he opened it to reveal her engagement ring. Her shocked silence lasted until he slid the three-carat diamond onto her finger.

"I've never worn anything so expensive."

"It suits you."

Her slender fingers appeared even more delicate weighted down with the thick band of diamonds. Roark rotated her hand and watched fire dance in the gems, enjoying the slight tremble of her fingers.

"It'll take some getting used to."

"The ring or me?"

Her lips quirked in a wry smile. "Both."

Before either of them saw it coming, he brushed his lips against hers, capturing her amusement for himself. His heart hammered against his ribs at her sharp *oh* of surprise. The texture of her lips fascinated him. He explored the plump contours with the same focus he might use when evaluating a precious artifact. This woman deserved to be treated with all the reverence he reserved for the things he pursued with such single-minded determination.

"Roark."

His name, whispered out of her, sparked his impatience. As lust sliced away at his control, he spread his fingers against the small of her back and drew her tight against his aching body. "Say it again."

She pulled back at his command, her torso arching. Passion-drenched and dreamy, her eyes met his. "What?"

"My name." He kissed her nose. "Just put a little more heat behind it." It was a dangerous request. His passion might be simmering now, but it wouldn't take much to push it into a roiling boil.

"Is this how you plan to be tonight?"

"And every night hereafter."

She rolled her eyes. "Roark." More a warning than a caress.

He hummed and shook his head. "No one's going to believe you're madly in love with me if you use that tone. Try again."

"Roark." Exasperated.

"They'll believe we're together if you sound impatient. But I had something more like this in mind." He cupped her face, snared her gaze and held her immobile with his steely will. "Elizabeth."

To his amusement, her eyes widened and her mouth popped open. He rarely spent time with women that couldn't handle his brand of seduction. Sophisticated women knew the score. Understood that he might be in it for the short-term, but that he would make it worth their while.

Elizabeth possessed an innocence that both captivated and

concerned him. She hadn't signed up to be seduced. And it was all he could think about doing.

"Do women fall for that?"

Her question shattered the sensual mood.

He frowned. "What do you mean do women fall for that?"

"The sexy voice. The take-off-your-clothes look."

No one had ever called him on it before. "I've never had any complaints." He cocked his head and regarded her. "Why aren't you falling for it?"

Her lashes lowered, concealing the secrets in her eyes. "Because I'm wise to your type."

"My type?" Unsure whether to be amused or annoyed, he prompted, "What type is that?"

"Bad boys."

"How is it you're immune?"

"Fool me once, shame on you," she quipped. "Fool me twice, shame on me."

"The best way to learn is by making mistakes."

"And yet I continue to make them. It's pretty apparent I have terrible judgment where men are concerned."

This intrigued him. She gave the appearance of a woman who knew exactly what she wanted and went after it. "Forgive me if I don't believe that."

"It's true." She twirled the diamond ring on her finger, but he could see her mind was far from the jewelry. "In high school, college and a year ago. The last one was the worst. I really believed if I loved him enough he would settle down and want to be a husband and a father." A harsh laugh broke from her, filled with self-loathing. "It was idiotic of me to believe he could change, that he might care enough about me to change. A scorpion is a scorpion. They behave according to their nature."

"If you want to get married and have kids why not pick the sort of man that wants the same thing?"

"Because those aren't the ones I'm attracted to." Her eyes were cool as they met his. "As much as I fought against it, I couldn't stop falling for unavailable men. The ones who don't show up when they're supposed to. Who forget to call you. Can't remember birthdays or special occasions."

Roark knew he'd been guilty of every one of those things at one point or another. How many women had become disillusioned with love because of him?

"But despite every disappointment, I didn't leave because occasionally there's a brief, exciting moment when he'd focus on me and for a while everything would be all right. And when the moment ended, I would spend all my energy trying to make it happen again. Eventually I decided that if the only man I want is bad for me, I'm just not going to be with anyone."

The shadows in her eyes bothered him. "I'm sorry those men hurt you."

She shrugged. "I let it happen. But never again. I'm done with bad boys. Done with disappointment. From now on, I'm going to focus on what I want. A fabulous career and motherhood."

And heaven help the man that got in the way.

Still disturbingly light-headed from Roark's intoxicating kiss, Elizabeth wiggled into the strapless silver sheath she'd bought for her "engagement" party, wondering what had possessed her to lay out her past romantic troubles for Roark. She could have acted the part of his fiancée for six months and kept things strictly business between them. Instead, she'd been so rattled by his seductive power that she'd been compelled to toss an overabundance of obstacles in his path.

She was a fool for panicking.

Flirting was like breathing to a playboy like Roark. As natural to him as following a scent was to a hound. She needn't worry about being the target of his chase. They had a business arrangement. She would just have to keep reminding him about that.

Hair up or down? She regarded her reflection in the bathroom mirror as she smoothed a comb through her blond curls. Did her eyes seem brighter tonight? Perhaps she was dazzled by the size of the diamond on her left hand? She admired the ring. Its heavy awkwardness on her finger reminded her of the weight of what she was doing with Roark. No one must suspect they weren't a happily engaged couple.

Could she put on a good enough show?

Lying wasn't something that came easy to her. Maybe if she simply lost herself in the fantasy of being the woman he adored. At least for a few hours a couple nights a week. As long as she lived in the real world by day, everything should work out just fine.

Or so she hoped.

Roark's guests had arrived while she primped. If she'd lingered overly long over her appearance, she could blame it on wanting to make a good impression on his friends. But in fact, she was grappling with her conscience and a minor case of nerves.

This would be the first party she'd organized where remaining invisible wasn't part of her job description. It was an odd sensation to walk into a room full of people and feel a dozen pairs of eyes bore into her.

As if aware of her discomfort, Roark intercepted her before she'd taken three steps into the room. He pulled her into his arms and kissed her lightly on the mouth.

"Breathtaking," he murmured, following up the first brush of his lips with a second, less fleeting contact. "Let's tell everyone to go home so I can have you all to myself."

His gaze gripped hers, deadly serious, but he'd raised his voice loud enough so those around him could hear. Elizabeth's heart jerked in her chest, but she pasted on a bright smile.

"Stop that," she scolded, keeping her tone light. It disturbed her how much she enjoyed his obvious desire for her. She couldn't let the chemistry between them flare. Playing along with his charade was one thing. Falling for his shenanigans would only leave her heart bruised when they parted. "What will your guests think?"

"That I haven't spent nearly enough time alone with you."

She put her hand on his cheek. "We can rectify that later."

His nostrils flared. Eyes widened in surprise and appreciation. He caught her hand and placed a searing kiss in the palm.

Like when he'd traced her head line at the wine auction party, her body burst into glorious life.

"I'm counting on it."

Despite the fact that she knew this was for the benefit of the people who'd been invited to the party so they could spread the word of Roark's engagement, for a couple seconds she had a hard time catching her breath.

Damn the man for being so convincing. She was starting to believe their charade.

"In the meantime, could you introduce me to some of your friends."

She knew her color was high as Roark drew her toward the first knot of guests. The next hour flew by in a blur of names and faces. Many she recognized. Keeping up on the society pages made sense for an ambitious party planner. A few she didn't recognize. About halfway around the room, Elizabeth realized Roark's guest list included almost all the board members from Waverly's. Since his goal was to put a positive spin on his personal life, naturally, his engagement party would include the people he needed to sway.

Given her coworkers' shock when she'd announced her engagement to Roark and their countless questions about why she'd been keeping such a juicy secret, Elizabeth had expected similar reactions from Roark's guests. To her surprise, everyone had greeted her warmly.

Well, not quite everyone.

Hostility radiated from a sultry, dark-eyed woman in her early twenties. She'd arrived late on the arm of an equally tall and striking young man who must be her brother—such was the resemblance between them. The exotic attractiveness of the pair snared the interest of those assembled.

"Who is that?" she asked Roark, indicating the beauty.

"Sabeen. And her brother Darius. He's the reason I spent the last three months in the Amazon."

Was it her imagination or did Roark sound disgruntled? "I thought you were there because you'd run into trouble with local drug lords."

"Darius ran into trouble. I went there to get him out of it."

"What was he doing in South America?"

"Looking for a temple I'd mentioned seeing years ago. It happens to be in a territory occupied by a very dangerous man."

"So, he's an antiquities hunter like you."

"No, he's not like me. He was after treasure that he intended to sell and become rich." A crease appeared between Roark's brows.

"Did he find the temple?"

"No. He was captured first." Roark grimaced. "I warned him what the temple held wasn't worth risking his life."

"Then why did he go?"

"He's in love with a girl. They grew up next door to each other in Cairo. Her father refuses to let them marry. He's ambitious and wants to marry his daughter to a very wealthy man. Darius hoped that by selling what he found in the temple he could become rich enough to change her father's mind."

"That's very romantic."

Roark shot her a dubious glance. "It's foolish. And he continues to pine for Fadira even though he can never have her."

"Maybe the father will change his mind."

"It's too late. While we were in Columbia, her father arranged her marriage. The wedding is set for the end of the month."

"Someone rich?"

Roark nodded. "And powerful. Sheikh Mallik Khouri of Rayas."

Elizabeth's head spun. "Doesn't his family own the missing Gold Heart statue?"

"Yes."

"Is this just a huge coincidence, or…" Elizabeth was gripped by a strong sense of foreboding.

Roark's expression was grim. "I don't know."

She mulled the situation, sensing there was something Roark was holding back.

"But Fadira's not married yet," she insisted, rooting for Darius to get his heart's desire. "There's still a chance for love to conquer all."

"It doesn't work that way."

Elizabeth could see she was wasting her breath trying to convince Roark that love wasn't a crazy, imprudent emotion. Her attention shifted back to Darius, and discovered Sabeen's gaze on her. Contempt flickered in their dark depths.

To feel that much hostility from a stranger put Elizabeth on full alert. "What about Sabeen?" Elizabeth cursed the tight tone in her voice.

"What about her?"

"Is there a reason why she looks as if she'd like to crush me like a bug?"

"Don't read anything into it. She can be volatile. I'm sure all you're seeing is that she's annoyed with me for springing this engagement on her."

Elizabeth searched his bland expression, sensing that he wasn't telling her everything. Did Sabeen's antagonism stem from jealousy? How close were she and Roark? What had Elizabeth gotten in the middle of?

"Why didn't you ask for her help?"

His lips twitched. Amusement brightened his eyes as his gaze captured hers. He lifted her hand to his lips. "Because I can't trust her."

The implication being he could trust Elizabeth. Her traitorous heart skipped in delight until his next words.

"She's far too passionate. She'd get swept up in the romance. I'd never get her to accept that the engagement was a business arrangement."

"She's in love with you." Elizabeth's spirits dipped.

He shrugged, but didn't deny her claim. "I knew her father for twenty years. He taught me Arabic and Persian. He was a brilliant man. Everything I know about Middle Eastern antiquities I learned from him. Before he died, he asked me to look after his children."

Only they weren't children. They were a passionate, sultry woman ripe for love and an adventure-seeking young man who looked like he was bursting with boredom at such a tame event as this.

"They don't appear as if they need looking after."

Roark's lips quirked. "Looks can be deceiving. Earlier this year I chased off a fortune hunter. She loses all common sense when it comes to love."

"Good thing she has you around to teach her how to be sensible." Elizabeth rolled the engagement ring around her finger.

"Are you trying to tell me something?"

"Only that you seem to have an overabundance of skepticism about falling in love."

"It's not skepticism," he retorted. "It's practicality. Few women are going to be happy with a man who's gone most of the year. They need constancy, want a partner. I can't provide either."

Was he warning her off? If so, he was wasting his breath. She recognized his type. Exciting. Challenging. But in the end, unavailable.

"And I'm not in the market for a man in my life," she spoke more to herself than him.

"So you say."

"So I mean." Elizabeth made sure he recognized the firm determination in her expression before she continued. "I won't deny you are exactly the type I used to go for, but those days are behind me. All I want now is to become a mother and excel as an event planner. I'm done with romance." With men, she added silently.

"Pity." Half-lidded, his striking eyes perused her body with sensual intensity. "I have plans for you."

"What?" A startled laugh escaped her at his bluntness. Her skin tingled as if he'd touched her. The sensation delighted her even as her mind scolded her for succumbing to his flirtation. "What sort of plans?" She winced at the husky timber of her voice. Damn the man for being so appealing.

A slow, predatory grin curved his chiseled lips. "Why don't you stick around after the party and I'll give you a preview."

Wicked man.

"Why don't you just tell me now."

"Because a demonstration is worth a thousand words," he

quipped. "And I think we would scandalize this staid group if I showed you what I had in mind for you."

"You seem pretty sure of yourself." *Stop flirting with the man.* "What if I'm immune to your charm?"

He brushed his fingertips down her bare arm, thumb grazing the side of her breast. She gasped. Her nipples hardened in anticipation.

"Are you?"

A ragged breath escaped her. "Apparently parts of me are not."

"It's those parts I'm interested in." He bent his head and kissed her cheek, his lips gentle and cooler than her overheated skin.

She was in trouble if he could set fire to her with nothing more than a series of provocative declarations. "And here I thought you wanted me for my keen mind."

"I like my women well-rounded."

Before she could reply to his double entendre they were approached by George Cromwell and his wife, Bunny. Despite knowing that impressing the socialite would help open doors in the future, Elizabeth had a hard time focusing on the impeccably dressed woman as she congratulated them on their engagement. Roark's right palm rested on her hip, his fingers cupping her curves possessively. His solid presence bathed her left side in warmth. Relaxing into his strength would be the easiest thing in the world. Her body was already melting against the hard planes of his muscular frame.

"What a beautiful ring," Bunny exclaimed, giving Elizabeth's hand a little turn so she could admire the diamond. She shot Roark a questioning look. "A family heirloom?"

"Only the diamond. It came from my grandmother's wedding ring. Elizabeth is a modern woman," he said, bestowing a wry smile on her. "I knew she would prefer a modern setting."

"A blend of old and new." Bunny nodded in complete understanding. "It's perfect."

As the conversation shifted to the inevitable questions of whether they'd set a wedding date and where they intended to marry, Elizabeth dodged specifics as best she could and smiled up at Roark, all the while hiding her dismay at the deception she'd allowed herself to become entangled in.

Roark must have sensed her disquiet because he gave her a gentle squeeze and kissed her cheek. "You're doing great," he murmured.

A second earlier she'd been ready to break free and run screaming from the room. With his words, some of her anxiety eased. And permitted her to notice a disastrous sensation. Delight. She hummed with it. Deep inside her, where an abundance of foolish inclinations frolicked, she was giddy over Roark's attentiveness and swamped with the longing to feel his strong hands roam over her body.

Her mind rebelled. This was the exact sort of thing she needed to guard against. Easier said than done.

After the party, when all the guests had departed and the catering crew had cleaned up and left, Elizabeth stood in the middle of the living room and told her racing heart to slow down. Every fond glance Roark had sent her way for the benefit of the board members had carried a sensual promise with it. Even from the opposite end of the room, she'd been caressed by his intent.

"Alone at last," he said, coming up behind her. His fingertips drew a line of goose bumps down her arm. His breath slipped warm and provocative against her neck.

"I think the party was a success." Was that her voice sounding all breathy and turned on?

"We achieved what we set out to do. The Waverly's board knows that beauty has tamed the beast."

Despite the way his fingers wandered along her waist with turbulent results, Elizabeth managed a chuckle. "I think I'd characterize you more like the big bad wolf."

He spun her around so abruptly, her mouth dropped open in a startled huff.

"Prepare to be gobbled up."

And his lips captured hers, robbing her of breath, torching her senses. It was magic.

A wave of longing crashed into her, drowning all thought.

Thank goodness his strong arm banded her body to his powerful frame or the weakness that attacked her knees would have left her puddled at his feet. She opened to his questing tongue and groaned at the sexy slide of his free hand over her butt. He kneaded her curves and lifted her against his hungry erection. Where moments earlier there'd been an unsatisfied ache between her thighs, a raging storm of desire shot from her heart to her loins. In the grip of fierce anticipation, she clutched his shoulders as he broke off the kiss.

His smooth lips drew a line of fire down her neck. "Sweetheart, you taste like heaven."

The intensity of his rough murmur thrilled her. From his playboy reputation she'd expected a masterful display of his seductive powers, not this hungry assault. His raw sensuality seeped beneath her skin, awakening the sort of primitive urges she swore she'd never give in to again.

In a flash all her past romantic disappointments came back to her. Her days of making poor choices were behind her. She had a plan. Career. Motherhood.

Elizabeth's willpower thrashed against the whirlpool of carnal sensation sucking her downward. With a deep breath she put her hands against Roark's chest and pressed. "I've got an early morning tomorrow. I really should be going."

And to her amazement, Roark let her go without a single protest. She chastised herself for being disappointed. No more getting involved with boys, especially the naughty ones. And Roark was as naughty as they got.

"Have dinner with me tomorrow," he said, catching her hand as she turned to go.

With his thumb stroking the erratic pulse in her wrist, she nodded. "Somewhere we can be seen together."

The suggestion was only half because they were supposed to be taking their engagement public. Now that she'd discovered the powerful chemistry between them, she had limited confidence in her ability to fend off his kisses. Worse, she couldn't count on her ability to keep her hands off him.

Even now, blood pounded hot and insistent through her veins, persuading her to put down her purse and garment bag and shove him down into the nearby nest of pillows.

"I'll pick you up at seven."

With a nod, she fled.

The cool night air did little to reduce the simmering emotions Roark's kiss had aroused. What was she thinking kissing him like that? This was supposed to be a business arrangement.

Elizabeth stepped to the curb to hail a taxi and caught a movement to her left. The rear door of a limo opened and Sabeen emerged. She caught Elizabeth's gaze on her and let her coat fall open to reveal her low-cut evening gown.

After a heated exchange with Roark, Darius had dragged his sister away from the party an hour ago. Why had she come back?

"I am surprised that you are leaving so early," Sabeen called, striding forward. "From the way you looked at Roark all evening, I didn't think you'd leave his bed before dawn."

The implication being that Elizabeth must not be able to keep her man happy if he was willing to let her go before midnight.

"I have an early morning." And now she was making excuses. "Did you forget something at the loft?"

"I didn't get a chance to thank Roark properly for returning my little brother to me unharmed."

Elizabeth had no trouble reading the sort of "proper" thank you Sabeen had in mind. At that moment, she felt sorry for the younger woman. No matter how beautiful or how hard she threw herself at Roark, he was never going to see her as anything but the daughter of his former friend and tutor.

"I'm sure he knows how much you appreciate his help, but go on up and thank him now. I know he'll enjoy seeing you. He told me you and your brother are like family."

She hadn't given Sabeen the sort of reaction the younger woman was hoping for. It was hard to be jealous when she was only pretending to be engaged to Roark, and she knew he wouldn't jeopardize the future of Waverly's for an indiscretion.

"And I will still be in his life, long after he tires of you."

Elizabeth didn't doubt that a bit. "Good evening, Sabeen."

Four

At three in the afternoon, only seven climbers scaled the rock wall at the Hartz Sports Club. With one of the most challenging climbing walls in the country and the largest in Manhattan, the facility was usually more crowded.

"You've been practicing while I've been gone," Roark called across to Vance, splitting his attention between his half brother and the difficult route he'd chosen.

"I wasn't going to let you embarrass me again," Vance returned, keeping his eyes on the wall in front of him.

"You should come with me to Pakistan and climb the Trango Towers."

Vance snorted. "I'm pretty sure I'm not ready for anything like that."

"How about something closer to home? There's Shiprock in New Mexico."

"Maybe when this business with Rothschild and the stolen statue goes away we can talk about it."

Roark nodded, sobering. For most of his life, the only family he'd known had been his mother. Then four years earlier, Vance had approached him with a tale of being his half brother. At first Roark had been skeptical. The story Vance had told him about finding a letter from his father that directed him to track down his half brother had seemed too far-fetched to be true.

With his mother's reclusive lifestyle, Roark had a hard time imagining her taking a lover. But Vance's story that they'd met when Edward Waverly had come to see her about a coin collection she wanted to sell made sense. Throughout Roark's childhood his mother had deflected all his questions about his father, leaving Roark to indulge his active imagination. He could see how his mother might have fallen in love with the charismatic Waverly.

But why had it ended?

Perhaps Edward had abandoned her after discovering she was pregnant. Perhaps she had broken things off because she knew she could never have been the sort of society wife a man like Edward would have wanted. Perhaps they'd just fallen out of love.

Roark turned his thoughts from the past to the present. "What are you and Ann planning to do about Rothschild?"

Vance stretched his left arm until his fingertips could just curve around his next hold. "We have to keep our stock price from dropping any lower. Otherwise we won't need to worry about board members selling to him—he will be able to pick up all the shares he wants on the open market."

"And the quickest way to stabilize the stock price is to clear up this mess about the Gold Heart statue."

Roark's thoughts ran over the questions raised by the FBI agents. He had no worries that Rothschild's machinations would land him in jail. He'd been nowhere near the palace on the night the Gold Heart statue disappeared. Of course, he couldn't prove that since his activities the evening in question were not the sort he wanted law officials poking into.

"That may present a bit of a challenge," Roark said. "The statue may bring in well over 200 million. With the theft of Rayas's Gold Heart statue the owner of our statue has grown quite paranoid about security."

"And you're sure it's neither stolen nor a fake?"

"I'm staking my reputation that it's not."

"You're staking the reputation of Waverly's that it's not."

"No, I'm not. Originally there were three statues created by the king of Rayas for his three daughters. Each one is marked with its own unique stamp and I have a document that distinguishes which statue belonged to which daughter. Currently, one statue resides with a branch of Rayas's royal family. The one the FBI believes I stole belongs to the current king. The last one disappeared over a century ago. Stolen or sold, no one knows, and the family has since died off. It ended up in Dubai and became part of a collection of a hundred other artifacts belonging to a wealthy sheikh who died recently. His son has little interest in anything old. He prefers cutting-edge technology, young beautiful women and expensive cars and real estate. Selling the collection is going to fund his dream of building the finest resort in Dubai."

"So when the statue arrives, you can prove both its authenticity and its ownership?"

"Exactly."

"Then we have nothing to worry about."

"Not a single thing."

Roark pondered the break-in that had happened in his Dubai apartment while he'd been in Colombia. The thief had disabled a state-of-the-art safe and stolen all the documentation Roark had on the Gold Heart statue including the statue's provenance. He'd made copies, but doubted these would satisfy the FBI experts.

He'd often been in situations where he needed others to trust him. Dealing in antiquities was the sort of business that came with a lot of questions. Black marketers thrived and the technology that should have made it easier to tell real from fake also made it easier to create replicas that appeared authentic.

For the next twenty minutes the men climbed in silence, each occupied with their own thoughts. As their hour ran down, Roark returned to the floor and unfastened his harness. As usual, climbing left his mind clear. When your life depended on the security of your next hand- or foothold, it was hard to clutter your thoughts with worrying about things you couldn't control.

"Your fiancée certainly made a splash with the board the other night," Vance said as he stored his gear.

"I'm glad to hear it."

Elizabeth had charmed everyone. A dozen people had informed Roark how lucky he was to have found such an exceptional woman.

"I had no idea that you'd gotten so serious with someone of late," Vance continued, his tone neutral. "How long have you two been together?"

"Not as long as you might think."

Vance must have heard something in Roark's tone because he glanced his way, eyes sharp. "She must have been worried when you disappeared for three months."

"It definitely tested our relationship, but she understands my need to be gone a fair amount."

"A fair amount?" Vance echoed, eyebrows raised. "It seems to me that you've been in New York a total of twenty days in the last year."

"Sounds about right." Roark focused on storing his gear. "But Elizabeth is very committed to her career. I'm convinced she didn't miss me at all."

"Quite a love match then." A thread of sarcasm wove through Vance's voice. Ever since falling for Charlotte, he'd become a champion of committed relationships.

"Exactly."

"Tell me how you came to be engaged." Vance drank deeply from his bottle of water, giving Roark a chance to decide what exactly he was going to tell his brother.

Deceiving Vance left him with a heavy conscience and a bitter taste in his mouth. Past experience had taught him to trust no one. That mantra had kept him alive more times than he could count. But Vance wasn't a shady antiquities dealer with questionable associates. He was a well-respected businessman and Roark's brother. Having family to guard his back was changing Roark from a solo operator into a team player, and adapting to the new dynamic wasn't easy.

"We're not really engaged," Roark admitted, deciding that

being truthful with Vance was best. "Cromwell approached me at the wine auction and told me Rothschild is after him to sell his shares and convince everyone else to do so, as well. He believes you, Ann and I are the future of Waverly's. But with the near scandal surrounding Ann's alleged relationship with Rothschild and my wild ways where women are concerned, he wasn't feeling confident about our judgment."

"That old man should talk. He's got more than a few skeletons in his closet."

As much as he would have loved to hear more about Vance's allegations, Roark stayed focused on his story. "Anyway, he thought if my love life settled down, I would demonstrate an ability to behave responsibly."

"So, you got engaged?"

"Elizabeth agreed to act as my fiancée until the situation at Waverly's stabilizes."

For a moment Vance looked mildly stunned, then he shook his head. "Did it occur to you that this is exactly the sort of thing that gets you into trouble?"

"Yes. But what else would you have me do? Waverly's is going to end up in Rothschild's hands if we can't keep our board members from selling. And you have to admit that the buzz about the Gold Heart statue being a fake or stolen has died down with the announcement of my engagement."

"Agreed." Vance scrutinized him a moment longer. "And speaking of you being the future of Waverly's, have you given any more thought to my proposition?"

"That I officially join Waverly's management and go public with our connection?" Roark shook his head. "It's not a good time."

"Don't be ridiculous. With Uncle Rutherford off doing who knows what, Waverly's needs you. Besides, you have the same rights to the company that I do."

"You seem to forget I'm the illegitimate son," Roark pointed out. "The black sheep of the family, if you will."

"I'm sure if my father had had his way, he would have married your mother." Vance picked up his gym bag. "He loved her."

"You don't know that." Not once had his mother named Edward Waverly in her journals. When she wrote of her lover, she talked about his thick brown hair and the unhappiness she'd glimpsed inside him. "And there's no proof he was my father." Despite the rumors, Roark never bought an artifact without authenticating its provenance. He was damn well not going to claim to be Edward Waverly's son without a declaration from his mother that it was true.

"The DNA test—"

"Proves we're related. We could be cousins." Roark knew his statement was ridiculous before Vance shot him a wry smile.

"You think you're Rutherford's son?"

"I don't know." Roark tempered his impatience. "And that's why I'm not keen on a public announcement."

"Fine. But I think if you come forward as a Waverly, it would go a long way toward bolstering our stock."

"Let's see how things progress with my engagement and I'll let you know."

Elizabeth swayed on her feet, half asleep as she waited for the elevator door to open. At seven o'clock on a Friday evening, the office housing Josie Summers's Event Planning was abandoned. Most of her coworkers were working events. The rest had left around five, eager to head home or swing by their favorite bar for happy hour.

Today had been a particularly difficult day. Not only because her newest client was a demanding perfectionist and unable to make a decision, but because she'd had a frustrating conversation with her mother about plans for Thanksgiving. With the number of parties booked around the holiday, Elizabeth couldn't get away from New York and she'd been unable to convince her parents to leave Portland and come for a visit.

Elizabeth really could have used her parents' support. A year ago she'd lost her sister, brother-in-law and niece. The ache of the loss rarely left her, but the pain had eased over the past twelve months. She no longer had days where it was nearly impossible to get out of bed in the morning, but not a day went by when she didn't see or hear something and pick up the phone to dial her sister. And now, it looked like she'd be spending Thanksgiving and the anniversary of their death alone.

Damn. Tears piled up in her eyes. She blinked away the moisture and willed the elevator to arrive. Already she was running late for her evening with Roark. He was expecting her at his loft in ten minutes. She'd give just about anything to be heading home.

They'd been out every night this week. Dinner with friends. A launch party for a socialite's shoe line. A special gala to raise money for diabetes research. And last night, he'd taken her to a Knicks game at Madison Square Garden.

Anywhere and everywhere they could be seen together.

As the elevator deposited her on the first floor, Elizabeth pulled out her phone and dialed Roark's number to let him know she was on her way at last. For a man who claimed to prefer an unfettered personal life, he'd demonstrated a protective streak.

At some point in the past fifteen minutes since she'd looked outside, a snowstorm had kicked up outside. Fat, quarter-sized flakes drifted down. If she hadn't been so darned tired, she might have enjoyed the beautiful scene. Instead, all she saw was the traffic snarled on the street before her. Catching a cab was going to be harder than she expected.

Flinching at the damage she was about to do to her favorite pair of shoes, Elizabeth pushed open the door and was surprised to see Roark's driver heading her way.

"Good evening, Miss Minerva."

"Hello, Fred." At the warmth of his smile, her throat tightened and tears sprang to her eyes. She was obviously more tired and overwrought than she thought.

"Mr. Black sent me to fetch you. He thought you might have trouble catching a cab tonight."

She gave him a watery smile. "I was just thinking that exact thing."

They'd agreed to meet at his loft tonight rather than have him pick her up at work. Until her day fell apart, she'd hoped to get

out at three, go home and grab an hour's sleep before heading
out for tonight's clubbing.

"Can you take me to my apartment so I can change?"

"Mr. Black requested I bring you to him directly."

And so she was being kidnapped. Elizabeth settled back into
the comfortable leather and watched the city slide past her window. The slow journey lulled her into closing her eyes. The
sound of Fred's voice awakened her.

"We're here, Miss Minerva."

She covered a jaw-cracking yawn with a gloved hand and
swung her feet onto the pavement. "Thanks."

Groggy from her short nap, she half stumbled across the
sidewalk and nodded to the doorman as she passed. When the
elevator door opened, she was surprised to see Roark.

"You were supposed to leave work at three."

Her heart thumped at his concern. She liked the way he worried about her. "Margo Hadwell is a demanding, difficult woman
to plan a party for."

He tugged her into the elevator and pushed the button to take
them to his floor. "You work too hard."

"I'm going to have to if I want Josie to make me a partner."

"How did your meeting with her go today?"

Thanks to Roark, when she'd approached her boss about her
future with Josie Summers's Event Planning, Elizabeth had been
ready to counter her boss's speculation about Elizabeth's surprise engagement.

"She swallowed our story that we met at a club the last time
you were in New York, and that we had a whirlwind affair. How
we fell in love by email. The roses you sent me after the Banks
wine auction helped sell it." Elizabeth grinned in triumph. "After
that, I was able to keep her focused through my entire proposal.
She agreed to bring me on as partner, but only if I land Green
New York's spring gala."

Sponsored by the largest conservancy organization in the city,
the gala was one of the must-attend events of the spring. Josie
had pitched on it three years in a row without success. This year
she'd challenged Elizabeth to do the impossible.

"Whatever introductions you need, let me know."

"Thanks, but there's more to winning the gala than just knowing the right people. I need to present the perfect proposal."

"You can do it."

Roark's confidence in her abilities raised her spirits. He'd been so supportive, exactly the way she'd dreamed the man in her life would be. Only Roark wasn't the man in her life. At least not in the traditional sense.

Filled with conflicting emotions, Elizabeth twisted the engagement ring around her finger as Roark opened the door to his loft. She needed to keep her head in this game and ignore the messages from her heart. And by the looks of what Roark had planned for the evening, that was going to prove challenging.

Candlelight illuminated the dining table, barely making a dent in the darkness filling the large open space. Soft music played. Intimate, romantic, staged for seduction.

Elizabeth swallowed hard. "I thought we were supposed to go out tonight."

"You sounded tired when I spoke to you on the phone earlier. I figured we'd stay in tonight. Have a quiet dinner, just the two of us."

She should struggle to free herself from the spell he wrapped around her so effortlessly, but his hand, sliding into the small of her back, and her exhaustion undermined her willpower.

"What about the club hopping we were supposed to do? You want us to be seen."

"We've been seen enough this week. Tonight, I want you to myself."

Treacherous delight stole through her. She cautioned herself to resist, but the intense light in Roark's eyes weakened her resolve. "Dinner sounds nice, but I'm so tired I might fall asleep over dessert."

A crooked smile bloomed. "Sweetheart, if I have my way, you'll be dessert."

His words seared through her like lightning, bringing her body to vibrant, tingling life.

"That's not funny." Her voice shook.

"It wasn't meant to be."

"Roark." Elizabeth's feet remained glued to the floor as he headed toward the kitchen. "We've talked about this. I'm not going to sleep with you."

"Don't make any decisions until you've tasted my lamb stew."

"You cooked?"

Honestly, how much more could one girl withstand?

"It relaxes me."

Without further argument, she let him tow her toward the table. The man was nearly impossible to resist. But she would keep up the battle until the last of her strength left her. She'd made a promise to herself. No more bad boys.

But was Roark as bad as his reputation made him out to be? Or was she fooling herself instead of confronting reality? How many times had she coated her doubts about a boyfriend in iridescent layers of hope, transforming ugly and uncomfortable truth into pretty falsehoods she could live with. Trouble was the bad stuff wasn't gone, only covered up by her optimism. Not this time.

"That was delicious." Elizabeth gathered their plates and headed for the kitchen. "When did you learn to cook?"

"Before I learned how to sneak out, I used to spend a fair amount of time in the kitchen with Rosie. Our cook." Melancholy settled over Roark as it always did when he talked about what it had been like to grow up in a penthouse high above the bustle of New York.

"What was your mother like?" Elizabeth looked contrite as soon as the words were said. "I'm sorry. If you'd rather not talk about her, I understand."

He shrugged. Talking about her had never been easy. His shame in leaving her the way he had was tied up in his resentment of how fiercely she'd sheltered him from the world, not understanding that an energetic boy needed activity and adventures.

"She was smart and tough. I never understood why someone

with her head for business and her iron will became like a terrified child outside her front door."

"Did something traumatic happen to her?"

"Not that I ever found in her journals." The square stem of the crystal wineglass felt cool against his fingertips as he spun the goblet and observed the play of candlelight in the facets. "She wrote about everything else."

"If she never left her penthouse, how did she…"

"Conceive me?" Even in the dim light, Roark couldn't miss the color splashed over Elizabeth's cheeks. "Unlike what we're doing, I imagine she had sex with my father."

Her lips thinned at his mild censure. "But how did they meet?"

Until Vance had entered his life four years ago with the tale that they were both sons of Edward Waverly, Roark hadn't realized how deeply he'd buried his longing for a father. The hole in his psyche had gone unnoticed before he'd left for the marines, but he now understood that it had been a persistent ache he'd learned to ignore. After his military career ended, he'd focused his energy on the hunt for antiquities and used the thrill of success to keep all disquiet at bay.

"My grandfather collected coins, some of them extremely valuable. After he died, my mother decided to sell his collection. She approached both Rothschild's and Waverly's. The representative from Waverly's convinced her to let him auction the coins."

"You mean Edward Waverly."

Roark thought back to the journal entry from that day. His mother's normally bold, confident penmanship had wobbled. Her crisp, matter-of-fact recounting of the day's events had become somewhat disjointed when describing her meeting with Edward Waverly.

"She never named him." Roark thought about those passages. He'd scrutinized them over the years, looking for answers to his father's identity. "A week later they were lovers."

"So fast?"

"When he saw something he wanted, he went after it." Roark

caught Elizabeth's hand and tugged her onto his lap. "That's something we have in common."

She made no attempt to hide her dismay. "Strictly business, remember?"

He bent down and kissed her tight lips. Almost immediately her spine lost its stiffness. Her hand crept over his shoulder and tangled in his hair. He smiled at her soft sigh of surrender. They'd been circling this moment for days, flirting with the attraction between them, testing the limits of restraint.

"Forget business," he murmured against her lips. "I want you."

Her body trembled. "I want you, too. But I'm not sure this is a good idea."

"This is a great idea. I thought so from the first second I laid eyes on you. Somehow, even from across the room I knew it would be like this between us. So damned hot."

He pulled her blouse free of her narrow skirt, fingers skimming past the silk hem. She gasped at the skin-on-skin contact. Her muscles tensed as he spread his fingers over her rib cage.

His lips fastened over hers, swallowing her groan. With tongue and teeth he explored her mouth. The taste of her, the abandon with which she kissed him back. He wanted more. So much more. And so did she.

Swirling sensation stole all rational thought. He focused all his attention on the woman in his arms.

Blood pounded in his ears, driving his need for her higher.

"Roark." Elizabeth shifted on his lap. Her chest pumped as she sucked in an irregular breath. "Your phone is ringing."

"I don't care." He nuzzled her neck and smiled when she quivered.

She got her hands between them and used his chest to lever herself off his lap. "What if it's important? You should answer it."

Cursing, he let Elizabeth back away, but held her gaze. "You're the only thing that's important to me at the moment."

The phone stopped ringing before she could respond. They stared at each other for a series of heartbeats, anticipation building once again. His palms still tingled with lingering pleasure from the exploration of her lush curves. His chest burned from contact with her full breasts. If pressing against her drove him wild, what the hell was going to happen to him when he made love to her?

He might never be the same.

Roark took a single step in her direction and the silence was shattered by another round of ringing.

"See." Elizabeth looked toward the phone. "They've called back. You'd better find out who it is.

He snatched up the phone. "Yes?"

"Good evening, Mr. Black," said the doorman. "Sorry for the interruption but the FBI is here. They want to speak with you."

Any hope Roark had of resuming their earlier activity vanished. "Send them up."

Elizabeth was watching him with a frown. "Should I go?" Her fingers shook as she stuffed her blouse back into her skirt and smoothed her hair.

"No need." He headed toward the door. "They won't be here long."

"Who won't?"

"The FBI."

She stiffened. "Nine o'clock on a Friday night is a little past regular office hours." Suspicion darkened her eyes. "What do they want with you?"

"There are some questions surrounding the Gold Heart statue Waverly's will be auctioning."

"What sort of questions?"

"Whether it's the same one stolen from Rayas."

"Is it?"

Her distrust cut him like the sharpest dagger. "No."

Walls slid into place around his heart. The guarded sensation was familiar and reassuring. Talking to Elizabeth about his mother had been like unlocking a vault sealed for centuries. Some things were meant to remain undiscovered.

"Why is the FBI talking to you?"

Roark knew he'd lose ground with her if he brushed off her

question. "Mallik Khouri accused me of stealing the statue from the palace." Annoyed with the interruption and frustrated by the suspicion that shadowed Elizabeth's eyes, he flung open the door. Voice dripping with sarcasm, he asked, "How can I help the FBI?"

"We've had some new developments regarding the missing Gold Heart statue we need to discuss with you tonight." Special Agent Matthews smiled at him from the hallway. Her lips bore a predatory curve.

Behind her, Agent Todd slumped in his ill-fitting overcoat, his expression sullen, appearing as if he'd rather be home on such a miserable night.

"Has the thief been caught?"

"Let's just say we're pursuing a strong lead." Agent Matthews's gaze flicked into the apartment and spotted Elizabeth. "Sorry for the interruption." She was anything but. A cat playing with a mouse. "May we come in?"

They were wasting their time. Until the statue arrived in America, they had no reason to arrest him. The theft had taken place in Rayas. That crime was for the authorities in Rayas to prosecute. However, trafficking in stolen merchandise would interest the FBI. Good thing he didn't do that sort of thing.

"Have you spoken to Dalton Rothschild?" Roark asked, still blocking the agents from entering the loft. "If someone stole the Gold Heart, he would be my lead suspect."

"Funny," Special Agent Matthews said. "That's exactly what he said about you."

"We'd like you to come in and tell us where and how you came by the statue Waverly's is planning to auction." Special Agent Todd didn't sound anywhere near as cordial as his words. They wanted answers and fast.

"I can't do that." The statement had more bite than he intended. Usually he was happy to cooperate with the FBI, but they'd interrupted a very promising interlude and reinforced the wall of distrust between him and Elizabeth. Roark exhaled and forced down his irritation. "I've signed a confidentiality agreement."

"How convenient," Agent Matthews drawled. "Let's go see if we can find something you can discuss."

"I'm not telling you anything."

Agent Matthews gaze moved past him. "Perhaps your fiancée knows something. Shall we bring her in and see?"

Roark ground his teeth. He didn't want Elizabeth involved in this mess. "I'll get my coat."

Triumph flashed in Agent Matthew's eyes. "You do that."

Although Elizabeth had remained in the kitchen, he had no doubt that she'd heard the entire exchange. The way she wouldn't meet his gaze as he neared spoke volumes.

"I should head home."

"Stay," he cajoled, cupping her face. "I'll explain everything when I get back."

"You don't owe me any explanations," she murmured, but the way she clutched the dish towel in her hands made Roark wonder if it was his neck she wanted to wring.

"Stay," he repeated. "I won't be long."

Her muscles softened minutely as he kissed her gently on the corner of her lips.

"Okay."

Satisfied, he returned to the agents.

"She seemed to need a lot of convincing to stick around," Special Agent Matthews remarked as they headed down the hall. "Doesn't she trust you?"

"She trusts me," he said as the elevator doors closed, trapping him in the small space with the two FBI agents. "It's you she doesn't trust."

"Really?" Matthews laughed. "And why is that?"

"She seems to think your pursuit is overzealous. Like maybe you've got the hots for me and this case is just an excuse to spend time alone with me."

Agent Matthews laughed, but there was no mirth in it. "She has no need to worry on that score."

"You're right about that. I'm a one-woman man and she's the one woman for me."

"From what I've heard, everyone is surprised by your engagement." Agent Matthews met Roark's impassive stare with her laser-sharp gaze. "Why keep Ms. Minerva such a secret if you two were so in love?"

"I wouldn't have pegged you as a fan of gossip, Agent Matthews." He accompanied his mocking words with a bland smile. "Do you have a pile of glossy magazines hidden away in your desk drawer?"

"I don't gossip, Mr. Black. I interview people for facts."

"And yet you're suspicious over the fact that I didn't flaunt my relationship with Elizabeth for the amusement of the New Yorkers that read Page Six."

While Agent Todd headed for the driver's side, Agent Matthews opened the back of the black cruiser and gestured Roark inside. "I'm suspicious over the timing of your engagement. It certainly has taken the focus off the Gold Heart statue."

Roark paused with his hand on the door and offered a sardonic grin. "What a cynic you are, Agent Matthews. Don't you realize that love finds you when you least expect it?"

Five

With Roark gone, the loft felt cold and cavernous. The man certainly filled a space with his charisma and sex appeal. She shivered.

What new information could the FBI have that would prompt them to drag Roark out of his apartment at nine o'clock at night? She regretted doubting him about the authenticity of the Gold Heart statue in his possession, but could he be protecting the true criminal out of a sense of loyalty to his old teacher? Had Darius stolen Rayas's statue?

Turned to ice by her thoughts, Elizabeth scooped a throw off the back of one of the couches and wrapped herself in it. The fat snowflakes drifting past the floor-to-ceiling windows drew her to the view of Manhattan.

Rampant longing continued to pulse in her loins. It shocked her how much she wanted Roark's hands on her, his mouth coasting over her skin. Her body ached with unfulfilled desires as she stared at the street seven stories below. If not for the FBI agent's interruption, she would have slept with Roark. What a mistake that would have been.

But even as the thought formed, the sentiment behind it was hollow. Elizabeth floundered in confusion. Either she was as misguided as ever when it came to romance, or Roark wasn't the bad boy he appeared to be.

Elizabeth turned away from the window. When had she stopped relying on logic and looked to her instincts for answers? His reputation, the trouble with the Gold Heart statue and the suspicions of the FBI should have given her more than enough reason to keep him at arm's length.

Instead, here she was, basing her decision to trust him on gut reaction. Granted, unlike other men she'd dated, not once had Roark acted in a way that undermined her confidence or made her feel insecure. But was she right to believe that he'd been truthful with her when his business dealings were questionable?

Emotions churning, she prowled across the living room's gleaming wood floors and trespassed into Roark's private domain. The last time she'd been in the loft, she'd been too busy with preparations for their "engagement" party to investigate the home of the man she was supposed to know everything about.

In fact, except for what she'd read in the papers and the little Roark had told her about his childhood, she had no idea about his interests outside treasure hunting and rock climbing. She knew he spent his days at Waverly's, meeting with Vance and Ann about the current crisis and the auction house's future.

The loft had four bedrooms in total. Elizabeth skipped the room she'd used to change the night of their engagement party and headed straight for Roark's master bedroom. No surprises here. White walls. A gorgeous oriental rug covering the hardwood floor. An enormous king-size bed. Dresser and nightstands in some dark wood. More floating shelves held vestiges of Roark's travels.

The lack of personal items and photos confirmed Elizabeth's concern that Roark was a man who wanted no ties, had no family celebrations to remember. He liked his freedom to take off whenever the next adventure called. And she was someone who had her days planned down to the minute months in advance.

Retreating back into the hall, she pushed open the door to

the room opposite Roark's and stared in dumbfounded surprise. Here was the heart of Roark's house. A cozy, cluttered space filled with wall-to-wall bookshelves, a chunky wood desk piled high with books and papers. Opposite her, an overstuffed chair sat beside an ornate fireplace.

She located the light switch and the lamp behind the chair snapped on, illuminating the spill of photos covering the ottoman. Curiosity pulled her into the room. She glanced at the books on the shelves she passed and noticed a predominance of history tomes. Most of these were ancient European volumes, many not written in English, and as she circled, she began to notice more and more on the Middle East. Then she noticed an open cabinet behind the desk filled with scrolls.

Without touching anything on the desk, she tried to see what Roark had been working on. Two of the three books that lay open were written in Arabic. Considering the amount of time Roark spent hunting down artifacts in the Middle East, Elizabeth wasn't surprised that he could read Arabic, but the fact that his notes were a mixture of English and Arabic intrigued her. It was almost as if he thought in both languages interchangeably.

Diagrams and doodles also filled the pages strewn across the desk. Roark was searching for another treasure. How long before his research ended and he was off on another adventure?

The depth of her disappointment drove Elizabeth away from the desk. So what if Roark left New York? She'd known from the first that it was bound to happen. No one could cage him for long, certainly not her, a woman playing at being his fiancée. But that she was sad at the thought of his leaving told her she was already in too deep.

Elizabeth found the switch that activated the gas fireplace and sat down in the chair, knocking the ottoman in the process and disturbing the stack of photos sitting there. Half a dozen slid to the floor. She picked them up, scrutinizing each. The last photo was of a statue of a woman, her heart rendered in gold. She stood on a base of more gold, stamped with some sort of seal. The statue Roark was accused of stealing. A hard knot developed in her stomach at the accusations lodged against him.

Restoring order to the photos, Elizabeth kicked off her shoes and curled up in the chair. She arranged the throw so it covered her chin to toes and let her head fall back. Gaze on the flames flickering a few feet away, she forced her mind still. In the weeks following the death of her sister, brother-in-law and niece, Elizabeth had perfected the technique of not thinking. If she hadn't she might have gone mad dwelling on all the ways she was going to miss them.

With her mind quiet and her body warm and comfortable, it didn't take long for Elizabeth's eyes to close. Sleep tugged at her. The week had been physically exhausting and emotionally taxing.

In the last moment of wakefulness came the tiniest tug of excitement. Her demanding, eventful week had left her little time to ponder. Now, as her thoughts slowed, she remembered why she'd risked getting involved with Roark. Soon she could start her next round of fertility treatments. Visions of diapers and pacifiers danced in her head as she drifted off to sleep.

She was awakened by the gentlest of touches above her eyebrow. The soft caress drifted down to her cheek and slipped behind her ear. She opened her eyes and gazed at Roark's face.

"What happened with the FBI?" she asked, her dreamy haze fading.

He toyed with her fingers. "They asked me the same questions as before."

"Did Darius steal Rayas's Gold Heart statue?" The question burst out of her, startling him.

"No." The corner of his lips twitched.

"You're sure?" She scanned his expression, unsure if she could read him well enough to determine if he was lying to her. "You said he needed money and he has motive to hurt the Sheikh."

"He's not a thief." He lifted her right hand and brushed a kiss across her palm. "I'm glad you made yourself at home. But you would have been more comfortable in my bed."

Firelight played across his strong bone structure, creating interesting shadows. Flames flickered in his eyes, causing parts of her to burn for him. Her breath grew shallow as a vise seemed to have clamped around her chest.

"And make things easy for you?" Despite the warmth of the room, she tugged the throw higher around her. "I thought you were a man who liked challenges."

"Getting you into bed isn't a challenge."

"You sound awfully confident about that."

As well he should be. He'd already proven how easily he breached her defenses. She might as well drop the drawbridge and wave the flag of surrender.

"I mean that I don't perceive making love to you as something I'm doing because my ego demands it, but because if I don't have you soon, I'm not sure how much longer I'll survive."

Elizabeth didn't know whether to trust his earnest speech, but his words struck the final blow to her guards. They became dust.

"Roark." She managed only his name before her throat locked up. But she'd always believed that actions spoke louder than words.

Catching his face in her hands, she leaned forward and kissed him. Beneath hers, his lips curved. She felt the muscles of his face shift against her fingertips and knew he was smiling. Happiness bloomed in her chest, an emotion lacking since her family's death.

She felt glorious. Rich and full. Awakening to the joy life used to hold for her.

Roark's mouth opened over hers as the kiss deepened. Her head swam as sensation overwhelmed her. She burned. Warmed inside and out by her need for this man. She craved his strength, his weight covering her. The touch of his skin against hers.

As if her hunger communicated to Roark, he slipped his hands beneath her body and scooped her into his arms. She clung to his shoulders. The throw fell away as he carried her from the room.

"Wait." She pushed at his chest as the cooler air from his bedroom struck her overheated skin. "Put me down. Please."

He heaved an enormous sigh, but did as she asked. "If you've changed your mind, give me thirty seconds to change it back."

"Thirty seconds?" She laughed, her head clearing with a little space between them. "Does your ego ever deflate?"

His smug grin bloomed. "Not until we're both completely satisfied."

He reached for her, but she backed away. "Stop." She sucked in a couple unsteady breaths and told her heart to slow. "I want to do this." She took stock of Roark, appraising his raw masculinity. A groan slipped free. "I really do, but you have to give me a second to clear my head. I took an oath, no more bad decisions about men. So, if I'm going to break my promise, I want to do so with my faculties fully engaged."

Roark stopped looking like a hungry lion and crossed his arms over his chest. Eyes narrowed, he met her gaze. "What does that mean?"

"Just stand there and don't move until I tell you to." When his eyebrows rose at her edict, she huffed, "Can you do that?"

He let one brawny shoulder hit the doorjamb and leaned there, watching her in silence. Elizabeth released a breath. Was she really going to do this?

She turned her back on Roark and grasped the first button on her blouse. The room was so silent she could hear her heart pounding. The rhythmic throb soothed her. She was going to do this and it was the right decision. Slowly, moving with deliberate determination, she opened her blouse and let it slip to the floor.

Roark would have traded the Monet hanging in his mother's bedroom to know what was running through Elizabeth's mind as she shimmied out of her skirt. This striptease of hers lacked any hint of sensuality. She was merely a woman taking off her clothes. Each move deliberate, slow, burdened with meaning.

The fact that she couldn't face him spoke volumes. Yet with each item she loosened and let slip to the floor a little of her tension fell away.

He was mesmerized.

And more than a little turned on.

Muscles played across her shoulders as she reached behind her to unfasten her bra. When had he last taken the time to just enjoy the curve of the female back? To admire a tiny waist. The flare of hips.

She wore lavender bikini panties. The bra that dangled from her fingers, the same matching silk. For the moment she remained immobile, her head down, studying the pool of fabric around her feet. Roark imagined she was torn between the need to neatly fold her clothes and whatever shyness kept her facing away from him.

The room seemed to hold its breath as he waited to see what she'd do next. The bra hit the floor, quickly followed by her silk panties.

Roark's lungs forgot how to work as she raised her arms and removed a series of pins from her hair. The golden honey mass plummeted downward, obscuring her shoulders and the top of her back. She shook her head and the waves shimmered in the lamplight. Then she stepped toward his bed.

Never had a woman captivated him the way Elizabeth had. Beautiful and smart. Wounded and vulnerable. It was an intoxicating combination.

In the silent room, his breath rasped with the effort to hold completely still. As much as it was killing him, Roark was happy to wait for her to signal she was ready for him.

She fisted her hand in the comforter and inched it back to reveal his sheets. Where she'd been moving slowly and deliberately until now, she quickened her movements and slipped into bed. Seated in the middle of his mattress, the cream-colored sheet tucked beneath her chin, she gave a sharp nod.

"Your turn."

Her dictatorial tone amused him, but he did as she asked. His fingers felt thick and clumsy as they worked his shirt buttons free. Beneath her steady regard, his already throbbing erection grew even more insistent. The frenzied passion of a few moments earlier had changed into something deeper, more dangerous. By approaching this moment with purpose, Elizabeth couldn't claim later that she'd been overwhelmed by physical desire. There was more to it than that. And Roark was eager to explore exactly what that was.

Removing his shirt, pants and socks, he paused to gather up her clothes and fold them neatly onto a chair before advancing toward the bed. She looked startled that he'd taken the time when his body so obviously reflected his acute desire for her.

Stopping beside the bed, he slid his underwear down his thighs, enjoying the play of emotions on her face as she got her first glimpse of what he had in store for her. "Ready?" he asked, gathering a handful of the sheet.

Her eyes were the deep blue of twilight as she stared at him. Her throat worked, lips parting, but nothing came out.

"Yes," she whispered at last.

Before the word was half out, he snapped his arm and tore the sheet from her grasp. A startled noise escaped her as he prowled onto the bed and bore her backward onto the waiting mattress.

"Oh, Roark." The cry broke from her lips as he gathered her hips in his hands and pulled her snug against him.

He sank into her mouth before she could speak again and ravaged her with long, sensual kisses. Teeth, tongue, lips all came into play as he learned exactly what pleased her. She gave him everything, held nothing in reserve. And her complete surrender unleashed something in him. Before he knew what had happened, he was devouring her in reckless, wild abandon, feeling her match his passion.

Panting, he released her mouth and drew his tongue down her neck. Her large round breasts filled his hands, tight nipples burning his palms. She moaned in breathless delight when his tongue flicked across one sensitive bud. The sound heated the blood speeding through Roark's veins.

Filling his nostrils with her scent, he savored the taste of her skin and let his fingers skim down her body. Her thighs parted as he skimmed over her mound and gently dipped into her hot flesh. Moisture spilled over his fingers. She was ready for him.

"I need you, Roark," she said, her fingers clutching his bare shoulders. Her eyes burned with fever as she bent her knees and opened still farther for him. "Don't make me wait any longer."

"Patience."

Stroking with more purpose, he circled her sensitive nub and watched her pupils dilate. Her breath seized, body jerking as he grazed her lightly before moving on. He wanted to know every inch of her before claiming her.

"Roark." Her desperation echoed his own driving need, but he continued to let his senses take her in.

"You are beautiful," he murmured, spanning her waist with his hands to hold her still while he deposited kisses on her abdomen. As he dipped his tongue into her navel and registered her startled gasp, he paused to reflect how one day soon she would have a baby growing inside her. With surprise he realized he'd like to see her belly swell with her pregnancy.

"Stop stalling and make love to me," she growled, squirming beneath him until he lay between her parted thighs. "I can't take much more of this. I need you."

"And I need you." Never one to deny a willing woman her pleasure, Roark kissed his way back up her body, pausing to drag his teeth across her nipples and further inflame her impatience.

Only when her hand closed around his erection did he appreciate the serious nature of her frustration. Fireworks exploded in his mind as her clever fingers stroked him. He shuddered at the enormous pleasure of her touch and shifted until he was poised at her entrance.

"Wait." He gasped as she shifted her hips upward and took him partway inside her. Sliding into her moist heat was the most incredible thing he'd ever experienced. She was so tight. It was acute torture to have to stop himself from driving all the way in. "You're not protected," he gasped, his lungs malfunctioning.

"I haven't been able to get pregnant with a doctor's help." Sorrow shadowed her expression for a moment. "There's no need for you to worry." And with that she lifted her hips and took him in fully.

As they merged he kissed her with something close to desperation. Breaking free of her lips, he buried his face in her neck and began to move inside her.

She matched his rhythm as if they'd been intimate for years. As her body shifted to take him still deeper, he struggled to slow the building pressure. He'd never expected her to be like this.

Unrestrained. Demanding. Her hunger a match for his. Nothing had ever felt so perfect before. He wanted to hold on to the moment, but already his body was racing toward its completion.

"I'm sorry," he said, refusing to finish until he'd satisfied her. "I wanted this to take longer, but you feel so amazing." He slid his hand between them and touched her most sensitive spot.

Immediately she cried out. Her body bowed. She scored his back with her nails, the small pain pushing him over the edge. As her orgasm claimed her, Roark surrendered to his own climax. It hit him harder than he'd expected, searing his nerve endings, knocking him off balance.

He lowered his weight onto her, becoming aware that she'd wrapped her thighs around his hips and appeared to have no intention of letting go. He cradled her cheek in his hand and kissed her tenderly.

"Are you okay?"

"Terrific." She hadn't yet opened her eyes, but her lips bore a satisfied curve. She dragged the tips of her fingers up and down his spine. "You?"

"Never better."

Reluctant to disrupt their comfortable intimacy, he rolled them both onto their sides so she was no longer bearing his weight. She snuggled against him, boneless and relaxed, as if she had no intention of moving ever again.

Which is why her next words came as such a shock.

"It's late," she murmured, her soft sigh whispering over his skin. "I should probably get going."

Six

In the glowing aftermath of their charged lovemaking, Elizabeth and Roark were using very little of his king-size mattress. Clasped in his powerful arms, her legs entwined with his muscular ones, Elizabeth wasn't sure where her heartbeat stopped and his began.

"It's late," he said, his tone brooking no argument. "Stay."

His lips moved against her temple in a contented fashion, mirroring her profound satisfaction. It was going to be torture to leave this moment of pure bliss. But to linger would open her up to hopes better left unexplored.

"Look, this was nice." So very nice. "But I think it's better if I go."

Elizabeth heard the reluctance in her voice and winced. He was going to get the idea that she didn't want to leave. And that would lead him to suspect other things. Like the fact that every second she spent in his company she fell a little further beneath his spell.

"If you insist on leaving, I'll take you home." With a fond hug he released her and shifted toward the edge of the bed.

She shivered at the loss of his warm skin. "You don't need to do that."

"If you think I'm going to let you wander around the city alone at this time of night, you're crazy."

Her heart did a silly little flip at his chivalry. Not one of the men she'd dated previously would have left a warm bed to escort her home. "I wasn't going to wander around. I was going to take a cab back to my apartment."

"At 4:00 a.m."

"You say that as if I haven't done it before."

His eyes narrowed. "You make a habit out of heading home at this hour?"

She could see where his mind had gone. He was trying to ascertain how often she'd spent half the night with a man and then headed home in the quiet hours before dawn. Her chin nudged upward.

"I am an event planner. That means I stay for hours after a party winds down. New York is the city that never sleeps. Sometimes that means I don't either."

"I'm starving." He tossed the covers to the foot of the bed, exposing both of them. "Let's get out of here."

His abrupt change of subject was almost as startling as the rush of chilly air across Elizabeth's warm skin. She squawked in protest, but Roark was already off the mattress and striding toward his discarded clothes.

She forgot all about being cold, and about her own nudity at the sight of all those amazing naked muscles that rippled beneath his skin. A purr rose in her throat. The man was a work of art.

He glanced back and caught her staring at him. "If you don't stop looking at me like that, I'm not going to let you out of bed for a week."

Heat rose in her cheeks as he perused her naked body. She slid off the bed and walked toward him. He'd already donned pants and shirt, but looked open to removing both if she insisted.

The purr rumbling in her chest intensified as she slid her arms around his midsection and hugged him. The move seemed to shock him because it took a couple heartbeats before his arms circled her.

With her cheek resting against his broad chest, she relaxed into the steady thump of his heart. "I really enjoyed myself tonight. Thank you."

She felt as much as heard his sigh. He tightened his arms.

"The night's not quite over." But he made no move toward the bed. The moment wasn't about sex. He seemed to get that. None of the other men she'd dated would have. With a gusty sigh he dropped a kiss on her head and pushed her to arm's length. "Let's go get some breakfast."

In ten minutes they were settled into a cab and heading uptown. Roark had his arm around her shoulders. Elizabeth snuggled into his side, delighted that he was sharing his heat with her. The temperature had dropped. Last night's slush had become rock-hard ice, uneven and treacherous beneath her four-inch heels.

Fifteen minutes later, the taxi stopped on Fifth Avenue in front of an elegant building. The entire block was residential.

Elizabeth scanned the area. "What are we doing here?"

"Breakfast." He tapped her on the nose, eyes dancing at her confusion.

"I don't see a restaurant."

"That's because there isn't one."

Roark paid the driver and stepped out of the cab. Elizabeth shrank from the hand he offered her.

He regarded her wryly. "Don't you trust me?"

Elizabeth pondered the loaded question even as she took his hand and let him pull her to her feet. "I think you enjoy keeping everyone guessing."

"Perhaps I do."

With a gusty sigh, she resigned herself to being surprised by whatever he had in mind. Her curiosity increased as he nodded at the doorman and escorted her into the building without being announced.

They disembarked from the elevator on the top floor and

he strode into the penthouse as if he owned it. At this hour, the lights were off, and the space had a vacant vibe.

"Who lives here?" she whispered, reluctant to disturb whatever ghosts lingered about.

"Mrs. Myott, she takes care of the place."

Roark flipped a light switch and illuminated the foyer. The gleaming wood floor of a long, wide gallery led the way into the apartment. A large fortune in artwork kept watch as Elizabeth let Roark usher her forward.

"And is this Mrs. Myott going to call the police when she notices us prowling around?" She stopped short in front of a painting. "That's a Monet."

"Yes." Roark's hand applied pressure on the small of her back, urging her on. "The kitchen's this way."

Elizabeth put her weight into her heels and refused to budge. "I'm not taking another step until you tell me whose apartment this is."

Roark shot her a mischievous grin. "Where's your sense of adventure?"

She let her raised eyebrows provide the answer.

"It's mine."

Another piece of the puzzle that was Roark Black snapped into place, but the picture wasn't any clearer.

"Yours?" This time Elizabeth was too shocked to resist when he nudged her into motion. "But you live in Soho."

"This is where I grew up."

"It's wonderful." The apartment's red damask wallpaper, antique furnishings and ornate marble fireplace might be the polar opposite of the white walls and contemporary furniture of Roark's loft, but the marble lions flanking the entry into the living room revealed where he'd come by his love of history and antiquities. "Why don't you live here?"

It was just a tiny flinch, little more than a twitch near his left eye, but Elizabeth noticed and realized that hidden beneath Roark's good-humored facade lay a thin layer of anxiety.

"Because I like my loft better."

"Why don't you sell it?"

"Want a tour?"

Once again he'd avoided a direct answer to her question. From the grin curving his lips as he imparted a tale about his boyhood antics, she could tell he was fond of the apartment. Good memories had been made here. But during one brief glance he shot her way, she spied melancholy deep in his eyes.

She could relate to the sadness. Her happy memories of her sister were intertwined with the aching reality that she'd never see Stephanie's face again or hear her laugh. They'd never stay up late talking about Elizabeth's job or the latest antics of Stephanie's book club members.

"And this was my bedroom."

Lost in thought, Elizabeth realized she'd missed a chunk of the tour. "Nice." She followed her comment with a grin. "Has it always looked like this?"

The large room, wallpapered in rich brown, was not exactly how she'd decorate a boy's room. A bed, canopied in heavy gold curtains dominated the wall opposite three large windows. The ceiling had been painted a dark turquoise, the color picked up in the two wing chairs flanking the heavy marble fireplace.

"I think it has looked like this since my grandfather bought the place."

Elizabeth rolled her lips in to contain a smile. "Not exactly your taste, is it?"

"No, but the bed's comfortable." And before she caught his intent, he swept her up in his arms and dropped her in the middle of the mattress. "When I was a teenager, I spent a lot of time imagining what it'd be like to have a girl in this bed."

Her thoughts melted into puddles of incoherence as he eased himself down on her and captured her mouth in a sweet, sexy kiss. Sliding her fingers into his hair, she lost herself in the feint and retreat of his tongue as it tangled with hers.

Despite the long hours they'd spent together, her desire for him rekindled, but he seemed perfectly content to take his time exploring her mouth in slow, tender kisses that awakened more of a tumult in her heart than in her loins. Last night she'd decided she could handle keeping their relationship purely physical. This affectionate intimacy was way more dangerous.

In the past few days she'd learned he liked her as well as desired her. It's why she'd decided to stop fighting the attraction between them. Trouble was, she was damned close to really liking him back. And therein lay trouble.

A throat cleared behind them.

"Welcome home, Roark."

A woman's wry voice cut through the romantic tension rising in Elizabeth. She put her hand on Roark's shoulder to push him back, but he'd already released her lips and set his forehead against hers. His chest pumped as he sucked air into his lungs.

From her position pinned beneath Roark, Elizabeth couldn't see the woman who stood in the doorway, but apparently Roark knew exactly who'd interrupted them.

"Hello, Mrs. Myott."

"I hear you are engaged." The caretaker's tone was so casual she might have been asking what he wanted in his coffee. "Is this the lucky lady?"

"Yes." Roark grinned down at Elizabeth. "Elizabeth, I'd like you to meet Mrs. Myott. Mrs. Myott, my fiancée, Elizabeth. I was giving her a tour of the apartment."

"And you decided to start with your bedroom. Is she impressed?"

Despite their compromising pose, Elizabeth was beginning to catch Roark's amusement.

"You'll have to ask her."

Cheeks on fire, Elizabeth cleared her throat. "It's very nice."

"Hopefully you'll approve of the rest of the house, as well."

Elizabeth poked Roark hard in the ribs, but although he grunted, he didn't move. "I'm sure it's lovely."

"Should I start breakfast?"

"Give us an hour," Roark answered.

"Very well."

The slap of slippers against the parquet floor faded as the caretaker headed off down the hall.

He didn't seriously intend to return to kissing her while Mrs.

Myott started the coffee, did he? When his lips swooped towards hers once more, Elizabeth realized that's exactly what he had in mind.

"Stop it," she whispered, wedging her arms between them. "We can't keep doing this. She knows we're here."

"She won't come back if that's what you're worried about."

"I'm not."

"Then what's the problem?"

And that's when Elizabeth shoved him aside and sat up. Roark rolled onto his back and grinned at her. The wicked light dancing in his eyes informed Elizabeth that he was teasing her. Well, it wasn't funny.

And yet, he looked so damned appealing with his crooked grin and his hair all mussed from her roving fingers, she almost leaned down and kissed him.

"A cup of coffee sounds really good right now," she said, ignoring Roark's smug expression. "Do you think Mrs. Myott has started some?"

Since she'd already tossed casual and unaffected out the window, Elizabeth scrambled off the bed in an ungainly assortment of legs and arms. With her feet on the floor, she smoothed her rumpled hair and tugged to straighten her disheveled clothes.

Roark came up behind her. Wrapping his arms around her waist, he nuzzled her ear. "No need to get all presentable on my account. I rather like you rumpled and out of sorts."

"I'm not doing it for you." She pulled out of his arms and headed for the door.

"You're doing it for Mrs. Myott."

"I'm doing it…"

"To make a good impression."

Damn him for being right.

"You don't need to worry," he murmured, taking her hand to lead the way when Elizabeth stalled in the hallway, unsure which way led to the kitchen. "She's going to love you."

"It doesn't matter if she loves me or not. We're not getting married."

"Then why do you care?"

"I…" She had an answer to his question, just not one she was willing to give him. So, she stole from his playbook. "Is that your mother?"

They were passing the library. His mother's favorite room in the house. Large and windowless, shelves lined every inch of wall space except for the large fireplace and the life-size portrait of Guinevere Black hanging over it.

"Yes."

Even though he knew it was little more than a trick of his subconscious, Roark had never been able to shake the sensation that her eyes followed him wherever he went in the room. He'd first noticed the phenomenon when he turned seven and spent long hours studying math, language, geography and history with his tutor. Despite her being elsewhere in the apartment, Roark always felt as if she watched over his lessons.

"She's beautiful." Elizabeth glanced his way. "You have her eyes."

"And her love of books." To his relief, the scent of coffee reached his nose. "Come on, Mrs. Myott has started breakfast."

"Why would she do that when you gave her the impression we'd be a while?"

He was growing rather fond of the way Elizabeth's cheeks turned pink and wondered what accounted for his change of taste. The women he usually dated didn't blush at the slightest hint of impropriety. When had he lost interest in audacious, free spirits? He appreciated their independent natures. Never worried that they'd grow too attached.

"She knows me." He wrapped his arm around Elizabeth's waist and guided her down the hall.

In the eighteen years he'd lived in the apartment, the kitchen had been a big, serviceable room meant to be a functional space with little aesthetic appeal. White subway tile on the walls. Gray tile on the floors. Stainless countertops.

Five years ago when he'd toyed with selling the place, he'd had the room renovated. Now, granite and slate in warm, earthy tones made the gourmet kitchen an elegant space to cook and entertain.

He guided Elizabeth onto a bar stool on the opposite side of the enormous center island from where Mrs. Myott cooked bacon on the six-burner stove and headed for the coffeepot. As he passed the diminutive woman with short, curly brown hair and keen blue eyes, he leaned over her shoulder and peered at the batter resting beside the heating waffle iron.

"Is there any of your famous strawberry preserves?"

"I put up a dozen jars this summer, all for you."

"That's my girl."

Mrs. Myott shot him a dry look. "I think you already have your hands full with the girl you've got."

"You have no idea," he murmured, fetching two cups of coffee and returning to Elizabeth. "I hope you like waffles. Mrs. Myott makes the best in New York City. And wait until you taste her preserves."

"Is there anything I can do to help?" Elizabeth asked.

"Not one thing. I made this boy breakfast for eighteen years until he ran off to serve his country."

"She was my nanny," Roark explained.

"Came to work for Ms. Black two days after this one was born."

Her husband had been killed during the invasion of Grenada in 1983. Roark remembered photos of her husband in his uniform, and the stories she'd told of the missions he'd gone on. It's probably where the first seed had been planted that led him to join the marines.

"And she stayed because by the time I no longer needed a nanny, she'd become part of the family."

"Your mother was a dear."

Elizabeth's expression was intent as she followed the exchange. "So, you have lots of stories from when Roark was growing up?"

"I do."

"That's not why I brought you here." His pulse hitched at Elizabeth's mischievous smile.

He reined in the urge to kiss all thought of teasing him right out of her mind. It seemed every time he turned around, he came up with another excuse to take her hand, touch her back, slide his arm around her waist and kiss her soft lips. She had bewitched him.

"No?" She sipped her coffee, eyes sparkling at him over the rim. "You could have taken me to any restaurant in Manhattan, but instead you brought me here. I think you want me to know every little detail about you."

Damned if she wasn't right. And here was the funny part. She had no idea that she'd just hit a bull's-eye. She thought she was poking fun at him when in fact, he'd just presented her with a tour guide to his past.

"No restaurant can compare to Mrs. Myott's waffles."

Lines appeared at the corners of the older woman's eyes as her expression softened. Nowhere near a real smile for the average person, but positively beaming for his former nanny.

While Mrs. Myott served up hot waffles and her delicious strawberry preserves, she filled Elizabeth in on some of the more entertaining stories from his childhood.

"Your poor tutor." The laughter in Elizabeth's velvet blue eyes belied her sympathetic tone. "What if he'd had a heart attack or something?"

"He was lying to my mother. I wouldn't care if he had." The exploding spring mechanism that Roark had placed beneath his tutor's coffee cup had dumped the hot contents into the man's lap. The way he'd gone after Roark had shown his true colors and not the polite face he presented to Roark's mom.

"You could have found a better way to convince your mother he was abusive."

"Yes, but none would have been as much fun."

The women exchanged a look. Their non-verbal communication was Roark's cue to get Elizabeth out of there. If they stayed much longer, there'd be no mystery left. And he needed to keep her intrigued with him. For a little while longer, anyway.

"I need to grab a couple books from Mom's library and then I'll take you home."

"Of course." Elizabeth smiled at Mrs. Myott. "Are you sure I can't help you with the dishes?"

"No need. This darling young man renovated a few years ago and I have top-of-the-line everything. It'll take me a second or two to clean up."

While Roark located the books he wanted, Elizabeth strolled up and down the hallway that ran from the gallery to the master bedroom. Seven feet wide and sixty feet long, the walls held some of the incredible artwork his mother had collected over the years.

"I could stare at these all day," she said when he rejoined her. "It's like living in a museum." She shook her head. "And yet, it's your home."

"My mother's home. I live in a loft in Soho, remember?"

"Why don't you move some of these there? Your walls could use some brightening."

"I'm not home enough. And your comment about a museum makes me think I should loan some of these out." Something he'd said had lost her. Roark felt her pull into herself. The camaraderie of these past few hours vanished as if it had never been.

"I imagine quite a few museums would be thrilled to display them."

Roark caught her arm as she turned to go and set his fingers beneath her chin to tip her face upward. "What's wrong?"

"Nothing." But she evaded his gaze. "I have an event tonight. I should get home and go over my preparations to make sure everything will run smoothly."

"Will you come over afterwards?"

She lifted her chin from his grasp. "It'll be late."

"I'll give you a key. You can wake me."

Her mouth dropped open. "A key to your loft? Why?"

"I should think it was obvious. We're engaged. You should feel free to come and go."

"Last night…" She stopped talking and rolled her lips inward. Her fingers knitted together in front of her. "I'm not sure I understand what's going on."

"Then let me make it perfectly clear. Last night was amazing.

I think you felt it, too. We have incredible chemistry. I want to explore it a whole lot further."

"I don't know. When I agreed to help you out, it was supposed to be a simple charade. Uncomplicated by anything physical."

"There's nothing complicated about what happened between us last night."

She gave him a you-have-to-be-kidding look. "Maybe not for you, but I have a bad habit of getting in too deep with men like you."

"Men like me?" Her generalization ignited his irritation. "What sort of man am I?"

"The sort who likes to take off without warning and views commitment like one step up from death."

He had no way to refute her claim. "And you want stability."

"More than that, I need to feel connected. To have someone I can count on. A year ago I lost my sister, her husband and my niece. They were killed in a car accident. She was my best friend. We talked every day. It's like a piece of my heart was cut out. Being alone is so hard. I'm afraid I'll start to rely on you and soon you'll be gone."

The pain throbbing in her voice lanced through him. He remembered the day his CO had informed him a call had come in while he was on training maneuvers. A thousand miles away his mother had died, alone and miserable because her only son had abandoned her.

"Of course I understand." How could he not. He had his own issues with letting people get too close.

Which left him with a conundrum. Making love with Elizabeth had been fantastic. He wasn't ready to give her up just because they wanted different things.

"Of course, now that we've slept together," she continued, "I'm almost guaranteed to start wanting more. It would be less of a problem if I wasn't so attracted to you or if you'd sucked in bed."

His mood lightened at her admission. "Then what would you suggest?"

She grimaced. "Just give me a little space to sort everything out. Get my head on straight."

"How much space?" He wanted her again. Now. He thundered with the craving to snatch her into his arms and plunder her mouth, to strip her bare and sink into her warmth. Hearing her admit that she had little defense against the chemistry between them was a powerful aphrodisiac.

"A few days."

"We have the Children's Hospital benefit to attend tomorrow night."

"Oh, right." She eyed him solemnly. "Can I count on you to keep your displays of affection strictly PG?"

He grinned. "Only if you promise to do the same."

Seven

"And this one?" Elizabeth drew the tip of her finger along a three-inch scar that transected Roark's right rib cage.

"An alley in Cairo." For the past hour she'd been cataloging all the damage done to his body, most of it in pursuit of antiquities, and Roark had explained every wound in the same matter-of-fact tone. "I'd gone there to get some information from a guy and ran into a competitor of mine instead."

It was close to midnight. Roark lounged in the middle of her bed, hands behind his head, lips quirked in a wry grin, his naked body laid out for her perusal. At the Children's Hospital benefit this evening he'd been respectful of her space just as he promised. No breath-stealing kisses. No provocative flirting. Just routine public displays of affection. His hand around her waist. His lips grazing her cheek.

And every second she'd grown more jittery with yearning. She knew he was bad for her, but her body betrayed her with every heartbeat.

"Dangerous business you're in." Her voice grated like a spoon caught in a garbage disposal. She couldn't match his nonchalance. She'd counted fifteen scars, nine from knives, five from bullets and one from a cigarette. "What happens when your luck runs out?"

"Who said anything about luck? I was trained by Master Li in Wing Chun and by the marines. I'm the Jackie Chan of treasure hunters."

She knew he was trying to lighten her mood, but now that she'd seen just how perilous his business could be, she was gripped by a familiar fear. *Let it go. He's not yours to worry about.*

"And if you're ambushed by ten burly men?"

"I'd run like hell to safety." Roark sat up and wrapped his arm around her waist. His free hand tangled in her hair, trapping her. His gray-green eyes had gone serious as he stared at her. "I'm smart enough to know when the odds are against me."

Her heart clenched. She wanted to kiss him hard and long, until the ache in her chest faded, but losing herself in passion would only stave off anxiety. It didn't solve anything. Hadn't she learned that?

She tried a laugh, but it sounded hollow. "I believe you think you're smart enough." She gasped as Roark's teeth grazed her neck. "I'm just not sure you know when to give up."

He tumbled her backward and let his weight push her into the mattress. Her fingers drilled into his hair. The texture was as soft and wonderful as she'd once imagined it would be and addictive as hell. So were his kisses. And the slide of his body into hers.

She moaned.

Her thighs parted, hips lifted and she found him hard and ready to drive her straight to the stars once more. An hour ago they'd come together in a frantic frenzy. Hands tearing at clothes, mouths fastened to each other as they'd circled and sidestepped the twelve-foot span from her front door to her bed.

It wasn't until he'd collapsed on her, chest heaving, that she'd thought to wonder if one of them had remembered to shut her front door. The thought of what a passing neighbor might have witnessed roused a giggle.

"Usually when a man is making love to you," Roark groused,

his long fingers enclosing her breast. "It's polite not to laugh at him."

She opened her eyes and caught him scowling at her. "I was just…oh." He'd sucked her nipple into his mouth and the wet suction blazed a trail of sensation straight down. The place between her thighs grew heavy with anticipation. She smiled beneath its weight.

It was easy to surrender to the moment with Roark kissing his way down her body. Later, she could fuss about the consequences of her actions tonight. Repeating that she had no intention of letting the lines blur between their fake public relationship and all too real private one made little sense anymore.

She might just have to accept that she was hopelessly infatuated with Roark and maybe even on the verge of falling in love. If she simply enjoyed their time together without dwelling on the reality that he would soon no longer need her, the next few months would be a lot more fun.

And the heartache that followed?

She'd survive. After all, she had lots of practice.

"You're still not paying attention to me." His tongue dipped into her navel and provoked a shiver. "I'll just have to do better."

Before she grasped his intent, he'd slipped lower on the mattress, his broad shoulders nudging between her thighs. When his mouth settled on her, Elizabeth cried out. The pleasure was so intense she stopped breathing.

Gathering handfuls of the sheets, she held on for dear life as Roark's clever tongue propelled her into a sensual storm. Her lungs seized. Her stomach clenched. The pressure built. Roark's fingers bit hard into her butt, holding her still as her hips began to writhe. And then she was flying, soaring upward like a roman candle. Exploding in the clean, cold air high above. Fragmenting into a million pieces that drifted back to earth on a peaceful, gentle breeze that cradled her.

"What was that?" she croaked, her throat raw from panting and screaming.

"That is what I'm going to do to you every time you aren't paying attention to me."

"I'll make sure I neglect you at least once a day."

Roark kissed his way back up her body. When he reached her mouth, he settled his lips over hers in a deep, penetrating kiss. As his tongue tangled with hers, he slipped inside her and groaned as his hips collided with hers.

"That feels amazing." He laced his fingers with hers and held perfectly still for a long moment.

Elizabeth set her feet on the mattress and shifted the angle of her hips to take him deeper. Roark obliged and then began a slow retreat. The friction revived her hunger for him and she began to move in time with his thrusts.

In the hours following the first time they'd made love, she told herself that sex with Roark had been so perfect because she'd been clear-headed when she'd made the decision to make love with him. She hadn't been seduced into it by smooth talk or her own insecurities.

But now she understood that what happened between them had a magical quality she'd never known before. It was as if they enjoyed perfect synchronicity. One body. One mind. One soul. She knew what he wanted without being told. He anticipated her needs as if he read her thoughts.

It might have terrified her if another orgasm wasn't approaching at the speed of light. Elizabeth dug her nails into his back and shuddered beneath the force of yet another massive climax.

"You okay?"

That he held off his own finish to worry about her made Elizabeth smile. "Perfect."

His face contorted with concentration as he pumped furiously and began to shudder with his release. She held tight while he spilled himself inside her, thrilled by the power of his orgasm.

In the aftermath, he snuggled his face into her neck and became a boneless heap. His absolute relaxation was at odds with the energy buzzing through her veins. Normally when she felt like this she cleaned her tiny studio, rearranged her closets or revisited her itinerary for the upcoming week.

Her muscles relaxed as Roark's arm settled across her midsection.

"Can I spend the night?"

She hadn't expected his request. Didn't know how to answer. And every second she hesitated, he shifted a little closer to unconsciousness. His breathing settled into a sleepy rhythm.

Elizabeth's gaze traced her ceiling. Contentment settled over her body, but her mind was a jumble of fragmented thoughts. Had her heart fallen into a familiar pattern? Was she closing her eyes to why she and Roark didn't work in order to savor how much she enjoyed being with him?

So what if Roark was wealthy. A scholar. Or that Elizabeth would never need to worry that he'd move in with her and then have sex with another woman while she was at work. That had been Philip. A struggling musician with a band named Puked Rabbits.

Tom was next. He'd caught her in a vulnerable place after she'd broken up with Philip and sweet-talked her right into bed. The day she asked him where their relationship was going was the last time she saw him.

Elizabeth shifted her head on the pillow and stared at Roark. She'd dated enough jerks to know that he didn't fall into that category. He might profess he didn't sell his mother's penthouse because of the memories it held, but she was certain he held on to it because it had been Mrs. Myott's home for almost thirty years.

Still, there was no question her taste ran to unavailable men. She'd long ago understood she was challenged by the idea of turning them into something better. She liked the idea of taking something anyone else would give up on and making it work. Like the loft venue for the wine auction party where she'd met Roark. Elizabeth had accepted the challenge after three other event planners had turned it down, intimidated by the magnitude of the transformation the loft required. It's why she'd gotten the job on such short notice. But she'd made it work. And brilliantly.

"You're going to have a hard time falling asleep if you don't shut your eyes," Roark's low masculine voice murmured close to her ear.

"I thought you were already asleep."

"I was dozing." His eyes opened and searched her face. "Your loud thinking woke me up."

"As if that could happen." But she couldn't make her expression match her lighthearted tone.

"What's wrong?"

"I was thinking about my sister. Wondering what she'd think about what we were doing."

"You don't think she'd approve." Once again, he'd read her like a professional poker player.

"Ever since we were kids she was my moral compass. Of course, back then I called her Little Miss Goody Two-shoes." Elizabeth swallowed the lump that had formed in her throat. "Everyone loved her. She never did anything wrong. Or at least she never got caught. That's what I was for. I got blamed for everything that happened."

"I could have used a little brother for that."

"Hard to believe she and I would grow up to be best friends."

"Would she have liked me?"

"Doesn't everyone?"

"I could put you to sleep counting all the enemies I have in the world."

She didn't like the reminder of the numerous healed wounds on his body. "Then, let me rephrase. Don't all the women you meet like you?"

"Pretty much. And you didn't answer my question."

"She would have liked you."

"You don't sound sure."

"She would have liked you," Elizabeth repeated with more conviction. "She just wouldn't have liked you for me."

Roark mulled over his reaction to Elizabeth's declaration as he let himself into the loft the following morning. Despite being fully absorbed in his thoughts, he immediately knew he wasn't alone in the loft. It was a disturbance in the air, a vibration that had saved his ass any number of times. Moving quietly, he plucked a sharp knife from a drawer in the kitchen and headed in search of his intruder.

His first destination was the study. Given the troubles over the Gold Heart statue, he expected whoever had entered the loft would start here. A regular thief would've walked off with the Matisse he'd brought over from the penthouse. It was his favorite of all the artwork and Elizabeth had been right to say the loft needed something on the walls.

The study was undisturbed. Roark frowned. He wasn't wrong about someone being in the loft, but if neither his research nor his artwork was what the intruder was after, was Roark's life in danger?

He crossed the hall and regarded his partially closed bedroom door. Did an assassin lurk behind it just out of sight? Heart thumping in anticipation of the fight to come, Roark reached out to nudge the door open and heard a soft sleepy groan coming from the direction of the bed. In his experience, killers rarely fell asleep while waiting for their prey. Roark shoved the door fully open and growled.

Sabeen lay sprawled across his sheets, black hair falling in luxurious waves over her naked back. She'd obviously slipped in during the evening with the idea of surprising him. What would have happened if he hadn't accompanied Elizabeth home? If he'd been able to convince her to come here for a nightcap? Granted, they weren't truly engaged, but he had little doubt Elizabeth wouldn't take kindly to finding a naked woman in his bed.

He wasn't taking kindly to it, either.

"Sabeen, get up and get dressed."

The young woman had been in the early stages of waking and Roark's sharp, loud demand acted like a shrill alarm clock. She sat up and clutched a sheet to her small breasts, but not before giving Roark a good look at what she was offering. He scowled at her. Her sleepy mind took a second to catch up to what she was seeing. A second later, her eyes went wide and her mouth dropped open as she stared at the knife in his hand.

"Roark, where have you been?"

"Making love to my fiancée. You remember Elizabeth, don't you?" Contentment rolled through him as he recalled the last several hours with Elizabeth. "She's the only woman I want in my bed."

Color flooded Sabeen's cheeks at Roark's rebuke, but her confidence never wavered. "She's too dull for you. You need a woman with passion. Someone who can satisfy you."

"Elizabeth satisfies me. More than any woman I've ever known." Roark had no idea what prompted him to add the second sentence, but he spoke the truth.

"You've never known me." She let the sheet fall and reached up to run her fingers through her long hair.

Roark felt nothing. For all that he thought of her as a little sister, she was an incredibly beautiful woman. But her nudity and seductive pose aroused him no more than a marble statue.

Time for a little hard truth. "And I never will. You are a child, Sabeen. Elizabeth is a woman."

"You don't love her. The engagement isn't even real."

Any warm spot Roark may have once had for his mentor's precocious daughter turned to ice at her accusation. "You don't know what you're talking about."

"Don't I?" Sabeen slid off the bed and stalked him like a jungle cat. "You forget that I'm not one of your stupid society friends, ready to believe any story you concoct. I know where you've been this last year and what you've been doing. There's been no woman in your life."

Roark scooped her clothes off the chair where she'd left them and tossed them her way. "Get dressed."

"Tell me you love her." Sabeen wasn't going to let the issue of his engagement drop until she received some confirmation of its legitimacy.

Roark wasn't going to lie. "My relationship with Elizabeth is none of your business."

"You don't love her."

"And you're such an expert?" In her attempt to goad him, she'd unleashed his impatience. "What about the business between you and that fortune hunter? When you looked in his eyes, did you see love or dollar signs?"

Gasping, Sabeen turned her back on him. Her hunched shoulders told Roark his point had hit home. Not proud of his counter-attack, he returned the knife to the kitchen and brewed a pot of coffee. As the dark brown liquid streamed into a glass pot, the blast of adrenaline receded. Weariness hit him. Roark rubbed his face and wondered how Elizabeth was doing. He wished he was snuggled beside her in that ridiculously tiny apartment she lived in.

They'd been hitting the social scene pretty hard these past ten days in an effort to establish the legitimacy of Roark's transformation from playboy into someone stable and responsible. Not that it was all for show. He might not want to tear up the town with a different woman every night, but that didn't mean the itch to embark on his next antiquity hunt was gone. Already the necessity to appear at parties and charity events chafed at him. He wasn't cut out to dress up and play nice. He'd rather be skulking through back alleys in Cairo or tracking down hidden caches in Kabul.

Only in the private moments he shared with Elizabeth did the restlessness leave him. Damn. He was on the verge of being domesticated.

"May I have a cup of coffee or are you planning on kicking me out as soon as possible?"

Roark poured a second cup and slid it across the counter toward her. Sabeen had dressed in black leggings and a short green skirt. A long black and maroon scarf, wound several times around her neck, almost obscured the black lace blouse she wore. Intricate gold earrings, Middle Eastern in design, played peeka-boo with her black hair.

She wasn't dressed to seduce. Her appearance in his bed had been an act of opportunity rather than premeditation.

"Give me the key." He looked at her purse. "Your brother has access to the loft so he can assist me when I'm overseas and need him to research something. You are not to come here without my permission."

She sulked as she fetched the key. "I came because I'm worried about Darius."

"So worried that you crawled naked into my bed?"

His point struck right where he wanted. She wouldn't look at him.

"The wedding is just around the corner. He's going to do something stupid—I just know it."

Concern buzzed. "The only stupid thing he could do is to help Fadira escape her father's plans for her."

And Sabeen's expression told him that's exactly what her brother intended to do. Cursing, Roark pulled out his phone and dialed Darius's number. It rolled to voice mail and Roark left him a terse message.

This is what love did to you. It made you stupid and foolhardy. Darius was going to risk his freedom, possibly his life, and for what? A pretty face. Some fleeting passion? Darius was twenty. Too young to have settled on one woman for the rest of his life.

Roark closed his eyes and imagined throttling the impulsive youth. Then, he refocused on the problem at hand and scrolled through the list of contacts on his phone.

"When did he leave?"

"Yesterday morning, I think."

Twenty-four hours. Darius could be in deep trouble already. "I'll make some calls."

"Thank you."

"I'm not doing this for you. I'm doing it for your father. I promised him that I would look out for you two." And the responsibility was like being trapped in a newly discovered Egyptian tomb. "I just had no idea it was going to become a full-time job."

Eight

The pre-sale exhibit at Waverly's had attracted a very select crowd. Elizabeth tried not to gawk at the who's who of New York society as she circled the room on Roark's arm. Although she'd protested against his purchasing the emerald gown she wore, Elizabeth appreciated that she'd lost this particular battle.

As she surveyed the collection of artwork, furniture and formal china that would be auctioned off the following week, the emerald-and-diamond earrings on loan from Roark's mother's collection tapped her neck. He'd refused to disclose their price or the value of the matching bracelet that she touched every few minutes to reassure herself it remained on her wrist, but she had the sneaking suspicion that what she wore cost upwards of a hundred thousand dollars.

Elizabeth glanced Roark's way. The man might be physically present, but his mind was a thousand miles away. He'd been distracted for the past two days, only abandoning whatever bothered him to make her body sing over and over. A tremor clutched her knees as she pictured the things he'd done to her in the hours leading up to the party.

Roark's phone rang, disturbing her sultry memories. He frowned at the screen and sent her an apologetic glance.

"Take it," she said, hoping the call would clear up whatever had been distracting him. "I'm going to get myself a glass of champagne and a plate of shrimp."

That he hadn't shared his troubles with her was yet another reminder that they were only playing at being engaged. It helped to slow the slide into falling in love with him. Or at least she was better able to brace for the eventual pain when she landed hard in reality. She pushed aside her concern and gave him an encouraging smile.

He answered the phone with a tight nod. "This is Roark."

The rest of the conversation was lost in the hum of voices around her as Roark strode toward the exit. This whole fake engagement was starting to mess with her head. Each time she behaved as if Roark owed her explanations, she drew closer to the moment when her expectations would lead to disappointment.

And she'd only have herself to blame.

"Elizabeth, how wonderful you look."

Elizabeth turned in the direction of the voice and smiled at Charlotte Waverly, the wife of Vance Waverly, Roark's half brother.

The woman was radiant in a white, strapless gown with an empire waist banded in silver sequins and a feather skirt that made the most of her curvy figure. Her long blond hair trailed over one shoulder. Diamonds dangled from her ears.

"I love your dress," Elizabeth retorted. "You look like an angel."

"Thank you, and your jewelry is divine. A gift from Roark?"

"On loan from his mother's collection."

Charlotte grinned. "A loan today, but yours the day you two get married."

Elizabeth's stomach twisted. More and more, any mention of her upcoming marriage was like a knife thrust to her gut. The longer this pretend engagement went on, the deeper beneath Roark's spell she slipped. Her worst fears were coming to light.

Losing Roark from her life would leave a hole in her heart as big as the state of Texas.

"Vance and I were hoping you'd join us for Thanksgiving dinner."

"Me?" Elizabeth's thoughts rushed to catch up with what Charlie was saying.

Charlie laughed. "Of course. You'll be family soon, and Roark mentioned that you have too many events that weekend to be able to get out of town to spend Thanksgiving with your parents."

Being swamped with work was what helped Elizabeth from crumbling beneath the weight of grief. Thanksgiving Day would mark a year since her sister and her family had died. Guilt stabbed at her. If Elizabeth hadn't been too busy with work to leave the city, Stephanie and her family wouldn't have been driving in to spend the holiday and they wouldn't have been killed on the road.

"That's awfully kind of you." Elizabeth groped for a way to refuse, but her throat closed, preventing any excuses from escaping.

"We'll have dinner around four. I'm so glad you can join us. From what Vance has told me, it's rare that Roark is in town, much less around for the holidays. Vance is looking forward to being surrounded by family this year."

A familiar arm circled her waist. "Mind if I steal my fiancée away? I have someone she must meet."

"Of course."

"You looked like you needed rescuing," Roark murmured. "What was she saying to you?"

"She invited me to Thanksgiving dinner." Elizabeth kept her expression smooth, but her insides were cramping. "Did you know about this?"

"Vance mentioned something about dinner, but it slipped my mind."

"I hate this."

"Hate what?"

Yes, what? The lies? The pretense that she was unaffected

by being included in a Thanksgiving dinner with his family? The fact that they weren't truly engaged and so she couldn't be the happy future bride with a wedding to plan? What a self-delusional idiot she was to claim that she was okay with never getting married, when it was why she'd always tried so hard in relationships even though it was obvious that the men she'd chosen didn't want the same things.

Elizabeth bit her lip hard to bring her wayward emotions back under control. The pain helped distract her from the ache in her chest.

"This time of year." She let out a ragged sigh. "My sister and her family died last Thanksgiving. They were driving down to the city to spend the weekend with me."

"Elizabeth, I'm so sorry."

His fingers covered hers. He understood about loss. And guilt.

"They wouldn't have died if I had taken the days off to drive up to Albany. But I put my career first and booked events all four days. Stephanie was determined I wasn't going to spend Thanksgiving by myself." Elizabeth gave a bitter laugh. "And now I'm always alone for the holidays."

"What about your parents?"

"Their life is in Oregon. They moved there seven years ago and have only been back once, when Trina was born." Elizabeth stared at the bracelet on her right wrist. "I suppose you think I'm being overly dramatic. From what you've said, you're almost never in New York for the holidays."

"They're just another day for me."

For a second she felt sorry for him. His mother had been his whole life. Growing up without brothers, sisters, cousins or grandparents left him without a support network to rely on. His old nanny was as close to family as he knew. But now there was Vance and Charlotte and her son. Only Roark didn't want to acknowledge his importance in their lives and theirs in his.

"Are you going to Vance's for Thanksgiving?"

"Do you want to go?"

He was giving her the choice?

"I know this fake engagement has been difficult for you," he continued. "If you don't want to spend the day with Vance and Charlie, I'll understand."

"I knew it." Sabeen came around the corner like a vengeful spirit. Attired in gold from head to toe, dazzling earrings, sparkling sequined dress, metallic sandals, she shimmered as she stalked toward them, her expression intent and malicious. "I was right that you didn't love her."

Roark met her halfway and seized her arm. The way Sabeen flinched, his grip must have been punishing. He halted her five feet from Elizabeth.

"You were eavesdropping?"

"I followed you to see if you'd heard anything from Darius." Her dark eyes flashed with malicious glee. "And I hear that you're not really engaged."

Roark gave her a rough shake. "This is for the good of Waverly's. You will say nothing."

Sabeen was one of those women who had a pretty pout. "Why didn't you pretend with me?"

"Because you would have seen it as something more than it is."

And he was counting that Elizabeth would not. She held her ground when everything inside her longed to flee the truth. She was in love with Roark. Despite her determination to stay strong, she'd tumbled head over heels.

"You and I belong together." Sabeen set her hand against Roark's cheek and stared up at him. "My father knew that. It's why he asked you to watch over me. He believed once I was old enough you would see me as your perfect mate."

Roark seized both her wrists and held her away from him. "Your father entrusted me with your fortune and your welfare. He expected nothing more than that I do right by you and your brother. This fantasy of yours needs to stop. I am not meant for you or anyone. Elizabeth is pretending to be engaged to me because Rothschild is trying to take over Waverly's and I need the board to be confident that Ann, Vance and I are the perfect choice for the future of Waverly's." He gave her a little shake. "Do you understand?"

"No." Sabeen tore free. "I love you. Why can't you give us a chance?"

Roark set his hands on his hips. "Sabeen…"

Before he could say more she backed away. "This isn't over."

Elizabeth began to breathe again as the brunette vanished the way she'd come. "Do you think she'll tell someone?"

"Who is she going to tell?"

Elizabeth pictured the roomful of New York society a few steps away. "I can think of a couple hundred people out there."

Roark's arm came around her. He lifted her chin and kissed her passionately. Elizabeth responded as if the past ten minutes had never happened. It was easy to forget everything in Roark's strong embrace. His lips transported her to another universe, a whole new dimension where her senses were in control and passion ruled.

"Don't worry about Sabeen," he murmured. His lips swept across her cheek and lingered near her ear. "She's just worried about her brother. Once she calms down, she'll forget all about what she heard tonight."

Elizabeth longed for even a fraction of Roark's confidence. The best she could do was press her cheek against his powerful chest and gather strength from the arms that circled her. He had more to lose if their masquerade became public knowledge.

"You might be underestimating what your rejection might drive her to do." Elizabeth pushed out of Roark's arms. She had no more claim to him than Sabeen and it was time she remembered that. "She's an emotional young woman with strong feelings for you."

"She's a girl who should be focused on finishing school and tormenting boys her own age."

Roark's words made Elizabeth shake her head. He might not have encouraged Sabeen, but he didn't understand how intoxicating his charisma was in large doses. And Elizabeth had been absorbing the stuff for two weeks now. She was hooked.

No doubt the young Egyptian girl had become addicted in a similar fashion.

Roark had been put in charge of her welfare by the girl's father. He'd rescued her brother from the Amazon jungle. It made perfect sense that hero worship had become infatuation.

"And if we stick to our story," Roark continued, squeezing her hand. "Stick together, it's the word of a hotheaded girl against the two of us."

Elizabeth forced away her anxiety. Over the next week, she was in charge of six different events, two of them last minute parties she'd scored thanks to the connections she'd made while on Roark's arm. All that meant she had enough to worry without loading up on Sabeen's drama.

"Is her brother really in danger?"

"He is unless I find and stop him."

"Is that why you've been so preoccupied these last few days?"

Roark cocked an eyebrow. "Have I neglected your needs?"

"No." She felt her cheeks heat beneath his loaded question. "It's just that you've been carrying your phone more as if you're waiting for someone to call."

All expression dropped from Roark's features. Worry shadowed his eyes. "The boy is a fool. He has gone to Cairo to steal Fadira away before her wedding. If he's caught, he could face imprisonment, maybe worse."

"Can you stop him?"

"If I can find him. I have friends looking for him now." Roark sounded annoyed and Elizabeth almost felt sorry for Darius. "And from what I discovered earlier today," he continued. "I'm not sure she'll go with him if he gets to her."

"Why not?"

"Her family is in trouble. It's why her father is forcing her to marry."

"Financial trouble?" Elizabeth recalled the reason Darius had gone looking for the temple in the Amazon.

"More like blackmail. He's trying to locate the documents that will exonerate her father and free her."

Elizabeth could see Roark was itching to join the action. "Are you going to help him look?"

"For now, I need to be here."

But she had to wonder how much longer before he took off on another adventure? Would he last much past Thanksgiving? Elizabeth scrutinized his frown and tense body language. She'd better prepare herself to say goodbye.

Roark was hanging by his fingertips thirty feet off the gym floor when his cell phone began to ring. This better be the call he'd been waiting for. Swinging his leg up, he slipped his toe into a hold and freed his right hand to tap the Bluetooth headset.

"Roark."

"I found someone who can help us find Mas."

Not the call he was waiting for, but just as good. "Where?"

"Cairo."

Not only was Roark searching for any word on Darius, he was tracking the thief who'd stolen the Gold Heart statue documents. "How long ago?"

"Two hours. Keeps a girlfriend in Agouza."

"Keep an eye on him, I'll be there in twelve hours."

Roark disconnected the call as soon as his feet hit the ground. He'd rappelled down the rock wall during the brief conversation and gathered up his duffel as soon as he'd packed away his gear.

On the street he hailed a taxi and dialed Vance. "I have some business in Cairo to take care of. Can you and Charlie escort Elizabeth to the gala tonight?" This evening's function benefited the local food pantry.

"Charlie and I will take care of your fiancée, but are you sure that leaving town is a good idea right now?"

"It's the perfect time. With all the suspicion surrounding the Gold Heart statue, I have to retrieve the documents that prove it's authentic and not the one missing from Rayas."

"And Elizabeth will be okay that you're not going to spend Thanksgiving with her?"

Roark shied away from the true answer. "This isn't a real engagement, remember?" The words didn't reflect well on his character, Roark decided. On this anniversary of her family's tragic accident, Elizabeth was counting on him to be there for her. She hadn't come right out and said so, but he'd noticed how much comfort she took in his presence. And wasn't that exactly what he'd hoped to avoid when he'd chosen Elizabeth to become his pretend fiancée?

"I remember," Vance said. "It's just that after seeing you two together I thought…"

"You thought what?" Roark interrupted, taking his bad mood out on his brother. "It's all an act."

"Well, it's a damned good one." Vance paused a second. "In fact, if I didn't know better, I'd say you had real feelings for Elizabeth."

"You don't know better. This is all for Waverly's. As soon as Rothschild's takeover threat is dealt with, I'm heading back to Dubai and Elizabeth will get on with her life."

Vance's words ate at Roark as he went to his loft to grab the bag he always kept packed for just such quick escapes before heading to a downtown Manhattan heliport. He'd already contacted a man who owed him a favor. To avoid being stopped by the FBI, he was hitching a ride on the businessman's Gulfstream to Amsterdam. From there he'd hop a commercial flight to Cairo.

Traffic slowed the taxi. Roark made use of the time to dial Elizabeth's cell. It went straight to voice mail. She didn't deserve to hear about his trip in a message. He disconnected the call. She was probably meeting with her boss. When she'd left his loft this morning, her mind had been far from her perfunctory goodbye kiss. Already they were behaving like a couple that had been together for years, taking each other for granted.

Yet, they'd only known each other three weeks.

Guilt nudged him, but he shoved it aside. Elizabeth knew what she was getting into when she'd agreed to help him out. He wasn't the sort who stayed put and enjoyed being domesticated. He craved the thrill of the chase. Wanted no one and nothing to pin him down.

Sure, this elaborate hoax to save Waverly's was a little unusual for him. But he wasn't doing it because he intended to stick around and get involved with the day-to-day running of Waverly's. That was Ann's responsibility.

Roark slipped his phone into a side pocket of his duffel and headed to the waiting helicopter that would take him to Long Island MacArthur Airport. The chopper ride would be too noisy for another try at calling Elizabeth. He would just have to wait.

The private plane was taxiing toward the runway when he finally made contact.

"That was a long meeting with Josie," he said. "How'd it go?"

"Much as I expected. She's determined the only way she'll make me a partner is if I convince Sonya Fremont to let us plan her event. What if I can't do that?"

"You could quit. Start your own business."

A long pause greeted his words. "Starting from scratch would take more time and money than I have."

"You have thirteen thousand dollars."

"You know what I'm going to use that money for."

They'd been around and around on the subject of her upcoming motherhood. In Roark's opinion she was too young to tie herself down with a child. "I'm sure there's at least one investor in Manhattan that believes in you and would be happy to lend you some start-up capital."

"I'm not taking any more of your money. Besides, I'm going to start the in vitro treatments as soon as Thanksgiving is over. I want to be a mom more than I want to be an entrepreneur. What I need is the security I will get from becoming Josie's partner." A thread of frustration ran through her voice. "But enough about my unproductive morning. Are you calling to tell me what time you'll pick me up tonight?"

"I'm calling to let you know that I'm not going to make it to the gala tonight, but I want you to go. I've already spoken with Vance. He will escort you."

"I'm not going if you can't."

"If you don't go you'll miss the chance to meet Sonya and speak with her in person about her gala." Over the past several days, she'd grown more melancholy as the anniversary of her sister's death approached. Leaving her alone on the holiday ate at him, but he needed to get those documents back.

"Very well. Why aren't you able to make it tonight?"

"I have a lead on the thief that stole the Gold Heart documents."

"You're leaving town?" Her voice cracked.

"I'm on a plane right now."

Silence greeted him.

"Elizabeth, you know I have to get the provenance paperwork back or the statue's only worth will be the gold it's composed of."

"Of course, I understand. When will you be back?"

"A few days. No more than a week."

"You'll miss Thanksgiving dinner tomorrow."

"I know. I'm sorry."

"It's fine."

But it wasn't. Roark heard a whiff of disappointment. They both knew it didn't belong there. Which is why she'd worked so hard to sound neutral.

"I hope you still intend to celebrate with Vance and Charlie."

"I'll make some excuse."

"They will be expecting you."

"They're expecting you and your fiancée." She let her point sink in for a second before saying, "Looks like there's an emergency with the Chapwell party. Stay safe."

She disconnected the call before he could reply. The jet raced down the runway, the momentum pushing him deep into his seat. They took to the air and Roark's stomach gave a familiar lurch. Land fell away as the plane climbed.

Unable to shake the sensation that what he was leaving behind was as important as what he intended to retrieve, he shut his eyes, but what played through his mind wasn't the mission ahead, but the night before. Elizabeth naked above him, her full breasts offered up for his possession as she rode him into a storm of pleasure so acute it had shaken him to his core.

With a silent curse he jerked his attention back to the present.

"Can I get you something?" A twentysomething brunette dressed in a crisp white blouse and black skirt smiled at him.

What he wanted was whiskey to burn away whatever this emotion was that ate at him, but eleven o'clock in the morning was too early for alcohol.

"Coffee. Black."

Might as well be fully awake to appreciate the waves of guilt rolling over him. For the second time in his life, he'd run from the most important woman in his life to pursue his own agenda. He hoped this time it wouldn't end as badly as the last.

Nine

The Waldorf-Astoria Starlight Roof accommodated six hundred and the room was half full when Elizabeth arrived on Vance's left arm, feeling distinctly like the third wheel she was. As kind as Charlie and Vance had been to her in Roark's absence, they were so obviously a newlywed couple that it was almost painful for her to be in their company.

After collecting their table assignments in the foyer, the trio posed for a photo. Elizabeth stepped aside, insisting that Vance and his wife should take one without her, and headed into the venue eager to gather ideas for future events of her own. Although she'd been expecting to be impressed, the room's eighteen-foot ceilings and tall windows draped in black and ivory gave her a momentary pang of envy. What would it be like to plan an event for a room like this?

Fifty tables of eight had been arranged in the long, narrow room. At the center of each table a thirty-inch pedestal arrangement of red roses and white delphinium offered a splash of color in the otherwise monochrome surroundings.

Elizabeth scouted where she'd be sitting before approaching

the open bar at the far end of the room. She ordered a white wine and stood in relative privacy away from the guests streaming into the center of the room. The table where she and the Waverly's would be sitting was near the podium. The food pantry was one of Ann Richardson's favorite charities and her work was being honored tonight.

Her heart began to pound as she spied Sonya Fremont enter the room. The woman had been in possession of Elizabeth's proposal for over ten days. As far as she knew no decision had been made on an event planner. Her future hinged on her ability to convince Sonya that she was the perfect person to handle the event.

Setting the wine down, Elizabeth started across the room in Sonya's direction. When she drew within ten feet, doubts closed in. What was she doing? Her only credibility at these sorts of functions came from standing beside Roark. Without him she might as well be invisible.

"Mrs. Fremont?" Where she found the courage to follow through on her initial impulse, Elizabeth would never know. "My name is Elizabeth Minerva. I'm—"

"Roark Black's fiancée." A dimple appeared beside Sonya's mouth as the petite blonde woman extended her hand. "The clever girl who tamed the city's most intriguing adventurer."

"I wouldn't go so far as to say tame." Elizabeth warmed beneath the woman's approval and relaxed. "I'm here and he's on a plane, heading to…" Had Roark told her where he was headed? She'd been so damned mad when he'd announced that he wasn't going to make it tonight, she couldn't recall if he'd said. She certainly hadn't asked. "Actually I have no idea where he's off to."

Sonya laughed. "Oh, dear, you've lost track of him already?" She linked her arm through Elizabeth's and turned toward the bar. "Not to worry. Roark is the sort of man who needs a long leash."

The notion of Roark putting up with any sort of leash amused Elizabeth to no end. "You sound like you know him pretty well."

"My husband has followed his career for some time. I think

he secretly wishes he'd run off on his own adventures when he was young instead of becoming an investment banker."

While Sonya flirted with the attractive bartender, Elizabeth retrieved her white wine and wondered how to broach the subject of the proposal. The room was three-quarters full and before too much longer everyone would begin to make their way to their tables. Her window would be lost.

"I suppose you're wondering if I've chosen the event planner for the gala."

Instead of groaning, Elizabeth applied a rueful smile to her lips. "Was I so obvious?"

"I figured it was high on your list when you approached me."

"That's a nice way of putting it."

Sonya flashed her a wicked grin. "I'm rarely nice. But I'm sure you know that. How is my old friend, Josie?" The very deliberate slur on the word "friend" took a sledgehammer to Elizabeth's optimism.

"She's fine."

"Still the same manipulative bitch she always was?"

"I…" Elizabeth felt the event slipping through her fingers with each question. She stood with one foot on either side of an ever-widening crevasse. "She hasn't changed much in the three years I've worked for her."

Sonya's laugh rang out. "You, my dear, should have been a diplomat. I like you very much. If you weren't working for my worst enemy I would hire you in a second."

"Please reconsider. I would do an incredible job for you."

"Did my old friend tell you what happened between us?"

Elizabeth's heart sank. There was bad blood between her boss and one of New York's most influential socialites? "No."

"Twenty years ago we were best friends. Two weeks before my wedding, she slept with my fiancé."

Elizabeth sucked in a shocked breath. Now she understood. Her boss had set her up to fail and since that was the case, Elizabeth had nothing to lose. "Please don't believe for a second that I'm unsympathetic to how much that hurt you, but keep in mind that for the last twelve years she has been supporting an unpub-

lished writer who has yet to propose to her while you are obviously very happy with a husband who adores you and can afford
to keep you in Alexander McQueen and Dolce & Gabbana."

Sonya sipped her wine and regarded Elizabeth over the rim.
"Are you always this straight-speaking?"

"Some clients like hearing the truth."

"Do they now?"

Neither the socialite's neutral tone nor her intent expression
gave Elizabeth any idea how her bluntness had been received.
"Others need their hand held and their reality sugar-coated."

"And you think I'm the former."

"I do."

"If I hire you can I expect more such truth from you?"

Elizabeth's head swam. She was so close to her goal that
it was hard to hold her breath and talk at the same time. "I'm
afraid so."

"Never be afraid of who you are." Sonya's head canted to the
side as she studied Elizabeth. "I like you. I'd like to hire you, but
I've sworn never to put a single coin in that woman's pocket."

"I understand." This is why Josie had made Sonya's event the
basis for her partnership. It was never going to happen. She'd
been destined to fail from the start.

"Call me if you ever wise up and leave Josie's employ. I think
we could make beautiful parties together."

"You'll be the first to know."

Leaving Sonya to work the room, Elizabeth pulled out her
phone and typed a quick text. It wasn't until she'd sent the message that she realized her first impulse had been to share the
results of the encounter with Roark.

With her mood further dampened, Elizabeth made her way
back to the Waverly table. She was the last to arrive.

Ann Richardson broke off her conversation as Elizabeth approached. "Where's Roark?"

Six pairs of eyes awaited her answer. Only two pairs held any
sympathy: Vance and Charlie. The weight of her fake engagement sat heavily on Elizabeth's shoulders. Irritation fired. How
dare Roark abandon her at such a crucial time. What was she

supposed to tell people when she had no idea what had prompted him to take off the way he had?

"He had an errand to run." The excuse sounded lame.

Ann narrowed her eyes. "What sort of an errand?"

"Hello, sorry I'm late." Wearing a bright smile, Sabeen appeared at Elizabeth's side in a strapless gown of cobalt-blue. "Roark called and told me to be your date tonight."

Given the tenor of their last conversation, Elizabeth wasn't sure whether or not to believe Sabeen. Roark had to know that having the young woman at her side during the dinner would increase Elizabeth's discomfort rather than ease it. But if Roark hadn't mentioned the gala, why else would Sabeen show up?

"That was thoughtful of him," Elizabeth murmured.

"And where is Roark?" Ann Richardson wasn't going to be satisfied until she had answers.

The look Sabeen shot Elizabeth was filled with triumph. "Didn't Elizabeth tell you? He's heading to Cairo."

Was that true? Roark hadn't shared his destination during their brief phone call. Of course, she hadn't asked any questions.

"He left the country?" Angry color flared in Ann's cheeks. "Without telling anyone? When is he coming back?"

"I believe a week," Elizabeth said.

Sabeen's lips curved in a feline smile. "He told me he planned to be back by Sunday."

Violent impulses stirred in Elizabeth as Vance and Charlie shared a sympathetic look. She neither needed nor deserved their pity. She and Roark weren't engaged, it was all a pretense. They'd known each other less than a month. It made perfect sense that he'd share more with Sabeen, a woman he'd known for ten years.

So, why did she feel so betrayed?

"And did he also tell you why he was in Cairo?" Ann gave Sabeen her full attention, dismissing Elizabeth in a way that made her grind her teeth.

All the problems with the Gold Heart statue had created tension between Ann and Roark. Elizabeth's resentment of Roark's abandonment grew as she took the backlash on her chin. More than anything she wanted to run away from this party and consume a quart of ice cream in her apartment, but she'd lose even more face if she did. Instead, she took her seat beside Vance and composed her features.

Roark's brother leaned over and muttered, "Roark didn't invite Sabeen to this party."

"You don't know that."

"He would never have done that to you. She took it upon herself to humiliate you like this."

Vance's words boosted Elizabeth's confidence out of the basement.

"Thank you."

Sabeen wore a triumphant expression as she took Roark's seat. Elizabeth let her have the battle. The younger woman waged a pointless war. As soon as the takeover of Waverly's was no longer a threat, Elizabeth and Roark would part ways, and he would return to his adventures. She wasn't Sabeen's competition. The world of antiquities procurement was.

While Sabeen drank glass after glass of wine and bubbled about a gallery opening she'd attended and a cat fight she'd glimpsed between two well-known socialites, Elizabeth nibbled at her salmon and willed the evening to be over.

The waiter was clearing her untouched dessert when she tuned back into what Sabeen was saying.

"And when he explained to me why he and Elizabeth had gotten engaged after knowing each other about a day, of course I forgave him."

Elizabeth's blood crystalized in her veins as Sabeen's words sunk in. The rest of the table seemed equally stunned as they stared her way.

"What exactly did he say?" Ann directed the question at Sabeen, but it was Elizabeth who took the brunt of her displeasure.

"That they'd gotten engaged because of the Waverly's takeover threat. One of your board members promised his support against the sale if Roark could prove he'd settled down enough to be an asset to Waverly's instead of a liability."

"Is this true?" Ann demanded.

Elizabeth was saved from answering by the head of the food pantry stepping to the podium to introduce Ann. Grateful for the minor reprieve, Elizabeth joined the clapping as Ann stood. Elizabeth went cold at the way Ann was staring at her from the raised platform. "You had no right to break Roark's confidence," Elizabeth said.

Sabeen tossed her head like a spoiled child. "How was I supposed to know he hadn't told these people? What's the big deal, anyway? He's doing it for them."

"And what if others heard you?" As soon as the words were out, Elizabeth could tell there was no reasoning with Sabeen.

"No one heard. You're just mad because you can't pretend Roark loves you anymore."

"Do you honestly think I have any illusions about my relationship with Roark? I'm not some foolish child who imagines that I can manipulate him into loving me by destroying everything else in his life that matters to him."

The tightness in her chest made her heart work hard for each beat. Her chair was too close to the table. The crowd of six hundred attendees sucked the oxygen from the room. Sweat broke out on her skin.

Ann's strong voice became a roar in her ears as Elizabeth noticed a woman at the next table wasn't paying attention to the speech, but was staring her way. Had she overheard Sabeen?

Anxiety crawled across Elizabeth's skin. If Roark had been here they could have faced down the gossip together. He'd have kissed her passionately in front of everyone and shut down the rumors that they weren't really engaged. Alone, Elizabeth couldn't rally the conviction to deny Sabeen's claim. All she could do was sit and try to keep her panic from showing.

But that took all her energy and by the time Ann's speech concluded, Elizabeth was completely drained.

She turned to Vance. "I need to go." She pushed back from the table and stood.

Vance got to his feet as well and put a gentle hand on her arm. "Charlie and I will take you home."

"No." Elizabeth shook her head. "Please stay. I will be fine."

Without a word to Sabeen, she headed for the exit, weaving her way between the tables. Her hands shook as she reclaimed her coat and slipped into it. The cold November air bit deep into her bones as she stepped onto the sidewalk. On the way back to her apartment her shivers grew in intensity despite the heat blowing from the taxi's air vents. By the time she'd stripped off her finery and crawled between the sheets she was convinced she'd never feel warm again.

The harsh midday sun bounced off the pitted pavement and stabbed at Roark's tired, dry eyes. He'd chosen a small round table by the window. A cup of coffee sat untouched near his elbow. Roark swiped at the sweat gathering on his forehead and scanned the traffic passing the café's open door.

Worry rubbed Roark's already short temper into something nasty. Smith was late. That wouldn't happen unless something was wrong. The ex-military man had an uncanny sense of time. Halfway through their first tour together, Roark had labeled him a walking timepiece.

His phone vibrated in his pocket. Roark's first thought was that Elizabeth had responded to one of his texts. He'd sent her several since arriving in Cairo, asking how her evening had gone. Her reply had been nonexistent. A muscle ticked in his jaw.

At first he'd assumed Elizabeth was still mad at him for taking off so unexpectedly and at a time when she most needed his support, but then Vance had filled him in about what had happened at the gala with Sabeen.

His gut clenched. The first thing he intended to do after returning to New York was show Sabeen what happened to someone who crossed him. After that, he was going to apologize to Elizabeth and kiss her senseless. Providing of course, that she was willing to see him.

Slipping the cell out, he checked the message.

Outside

Cryptic bastard. The text was from Smith, not Elizabeth. Disappointment sliced razor sharp. He reminded himself that it was a little after noon in Cairo, 5:00 a.m. in New York. Elizabeth probably wouldn't be up for another couple of hours.

Shoving the phone back into his pocket, Roark headed for the exit. Had he really expected that she'd be quick to forgive him after facing the exposure of their masquerade all by herself? Granted, Sabeen had only told Roark's family and Ann Richardson. The story wouldn't spread beyond them, but Ann couldn't have taken the news well. And Elizabeth shouldn't have had to face everyone alone.

Roark stepped from the café and spotted Smith leaning against the passenger door of a rusty brown Toyota, enormous biceps crossed over a powerful chest.

The six-foot-four-inch former marine pushed away from the car as Roark neared. "Get in."

"Where are we going?"

"Somewhere quiet."

Another thing about Smith was his brevity. The man rarely strung more than four words together at a time. While Smith negotiated the Cairo traffic, Roark sent Elizabeth another text.

"Trouble?" Smith inquired.

Roark put the phone away. "Yeah."

"What kind?"

"Female."

Smith grunted. "Not like you."

"This one's different."

Smith let one raised eyebrow speak for him.

"She's doing me a favor and it landed her in some hot water."

"Sleeping with her?"

This time it was Roark who let his expression do the talking.

Smith's thin lips twitched. "Idiot."

"Shut up."

And that was last the two men spoke until Smith popped the car trunk. "Got Masler's fence."

They were alone in an empty warehouse on the outskirts of Old Cairo. The building was practically falling down around them, but for whatever Smith had in mind, this was the perfect location.

"Does he know where Masler is?"

"Let's find out."

The two men pulled the terrified Egyptian out of the trunk and set him on his feet, keeping a hold on his arms as he swayed unsteadily. Beneath his olive complexion, the man was green. Roark understood why. Smith's driving through Cairo involved short bursts of acceleration, followed by hard braking and frequent lane changes. The fence had probably gotten pretty scrambled. Roark only hoped the guy retained enough of his faculties to assist them.

"I'm not telling you anything," the fence declared after Smith shoved him into a chair.

Roark had just finished securing their captive's legs and arms when a plain black car entered the warehouse. Adrenaline spiking, Roark cursed the intrusion, but Smith's only reaction was to shoot the vehicle a look of disgust. Vigilance easing, Roark slid the hunting knife with its six-inch blade back into its sheath inside his boot.

"You're late," Smith said to the man approaching them.

He was about a head shorter than Smith and wore a navy windbreaker emblazoned with an Interpol emblem. "You said one o'clock. It's five after."

Smith grunted a reply and handed a camera to Roark, and a beer to the Interpol agent. Before the fence knew what they were about, the Interpol agent goosed him in the ribs, producing a somewhat lively expression and Roark caught the two men in a celebratory moment. After a quick check to make sure he'd gotten the shot they needed, he handed the camera off to Smith who uploaded the photo on to his laptop.

"Nice," Smith remarked and tossed a fat envelope toward the agent. "Thanks."

Without checking its contents, the man from Interpol pocketed the envelope. "Call me when you track down Masler."

"Will do."

Roark stared at the fence while Smith clicked away on the computer. It took a lot of willpower not to grin at the terrified Egyptian. "My friend here is uploading that photo of you and an Interpol agent even as we speak." He glanced toward Smith. "Where are you posting it?"

"His Facebook page."

The man's dark eyes showed white all around. "I don't have a Facebook page."

"You do now. I'm sure Masler is going to be very unhappy to see you being so chummy with your new Interpol buddy. Not to mention how the rest of your clients will react."

"It will ruin me."

"It will get you killed."

"Or worse," Smith added as Roark watched the man's composure fragment.

"Yes, killed." The fence nodded vigorously, a bead of sweat sliding down his temple. "They will kill me. You cannot do this."

"Maybe you should tweet about it while you're at it. Hashtag snitch." Keeping his gaze glued on the fence, Roark tossed the suggestion over his shoulder. "I've heard Masler follows Interpol."

Obviously it never occurred to the panicky fence that someone in Masler's business stayed miles away from any sort of social networking. His gaze bounced between Smith and Roark, agitation growing by the second.

"Stop," the fence cried, clearly at the end of his rope. "I'll tell you how to find Masler."

Smith stopped typing and stared at the man in the chair, his finger hovering over the laptop. "Speak."

An hour later, Smith and Roark dumped the man a mile from his home and then drove to Roark's hotel.

Inside the hotel room, Roark asked over a passable single malt, "Think he'll warn Masler we're on to him?"

Smith tossed his back in one swallow and poured a second. "Doubtful."

That meant he could set a trap for Masler and bait it with something the thief would find irresistible like the second leopard statue. Smith finished his second shot with the same efficiency as the first and headed toward the door.

"Thanks for your help on this," Roark called after him. "And let me know when you locate Darius."

"Will do." Smith paused halfway out the door and turned back. "This girl, she good for you?"

Smith's question caught Roark off guard. His first impulse was to toss off a careless answer, but after what his buddy had done for him both today and in the past, Roark decided he owed him better than that.

"Very good."

"Love her?"

"Don't know."

Smith shook his head. "Idiot."

"Yeah." Roark sighed as the door closed on his friend. "Damn straight."

Ten

Elizabeth's hand hovered over the pint of ice cream in her freezer. At seven in the morning, it was too early for her to get started, but today's Page Six article gave her a solid excuse to indulge in Cherry Garcia.

Her first phone call this morning had come from Allison, warning her that Sabeen's indiscretion last night had indeed been overheard. That call had been followed by one from Charlotte and three from Josie. Elizabeth had let those calls go to voice mail. After speaking to Allison, she'd been unable to face anyone else.

Shutting the freezer door before she surrendered to self-destructive eating, she took her phone back to bed. Curled beneath the warm comforter, she scanned through the dozen texts Roark had sent her the previous night. As low as she felt at the moment, reading the messages gave her mood a minor boost. In his autocratic way, Roark did appear somewhat remorseful that he'd abandoned her to the wolves. But this was his fight to wage, not hers, and just because he was conveniently missing in action didn't mean she had to be the one to clean up his mess.

An hour later she grew tired of moping and decided to bake the pumpkin pie she'd intended to bring to Thanksgiving dinner at Vance and Charlie's home. After reading the Page Six article, there was no way she was leaving her apartment, but no reason why she couldn't celebrate the holiday.

She was rolling out the pie dough when her doorbell rang. Dusting flour from her hands, she headed to the front door. Josie stood in the hall.

"I suppose you thought to make a fool of me by pretending to be engaged to Roark Black," her boss began without even a hello. "Well, I'm here to tell you that not only am I never going to make you a partner, but you're fired, as well."

On the heels of everything else that had happened in the last twenty-four hours, Elizabeth saw Josie's pinched mouth and accusatory, close-set eyes through a glaze of red. "Fine. Then I guess I'll be opening my own event planning company. And my first client will be Sonya Fremont. She's agreed to let me plan her gala."

The sheer insanity of the boast shocked Elizabeth out of her fury. She had no idea if Sonya would even agree to take her call once she read the Page Six story. For that matter, Elizabeth had no idea if any of the society women who'd hired her would let her continue working on their projects.

Josie's mouth opened and closed. She looked thunderstruck. "Sonya agreed to hire us?"

"She agreed to hire *me*," Elizabeth corrected, emphasizing the last word. Or she prayed that Sonya's offer still stood. "She refuses to have anything to do with you."

Having an important client like Sonya Fremont would make it easy enough for Elizabeth to find a job with another event planner.

"I can't believe you'd turn on me like this," Josie said. "After everything I did for you."

"You fired me." Granted, Elizabeth hadn't gotten a full night's sleep, but was she hearing things or had her boss fired her thirty seconds earlier. "How have I turned on you?"

"You said terrible things to Sonya about me, didn't you? That's why she won't work with me."

"I didn't say anything to Sonya about you." What the hell had she been thinking to continue working for someone as crazy as Josie?

"What about your events this weekend? Are you planning on abandoning all of those, as well?"

"I guess you should have thought about that before you fired me."

As she shut the door in her boss's face, Josie's last words struck her. "I'm going to make sure that no other event planners will dare touch you," Josie yelled, her voice carrying loud and clear through the door. "You're going to rue the day you messed with me."

Rue the day?

Between her former boss's poison and the outing of her pretend engagement to Roark, what if Elizabeth couldn't find another job? Earlier in the week she'd gone to the fertility clinic to have blood work done in the hopes that she could start the process towards another in vitro attempt. The third round had to be the charm. But if she had no job, it wouldn't matter if Roark's money helped her get pregnant—she wouldn't be able to support a child on unemployment.

Covering her mouth with both hands, Elizabeth set her back against the door as her knees gave way. She slid down the door. When her butt hit the floor she collapsed in a fit of giggles. It wasn't until she was gasping for breath that she realized she was crying. Yep, it was official, she'd hit rock bottom.

On the one-year anniversary of the worst day of her life, she'd celebrated by becoming a social pariah and slamming the door in her boss's face instead of begging for her job back. It was perfect.

From her nightstand came the sound of her cell phone. Elizabeth wiped tears from her cheeks with the back of her hands and pushed off the floor. On the television, Garfield the cat floated into Times Square. Elizabeth had surrounded herself with all her favorite Thanksgiving traditions, but no cheer filled the hollow in her chest.

She didn't get to the phone before it rolled to voice mail. It was Roark.

"Elizabeth, Vance called and told me we hit Page Six. I'm sorry I'm not there to handle this, but I'm catching the first plane home. In the meantime, it would be best if you don't speak to any reporters or talk to anyone. That might make things worse. I'll deal with everything when I get back."

His voice sounded brisk and authoritative, an employer gearing up for damage control. Yet another reminder that they weren't in this as a couple, but as coconspirators. Still, it would be nice to feel his arms around her. To be able to lean on him.

Elizabeth shook off her unrealistic longing and went back to her pie. By the time it went into the oven, her kitchen was covered in a thin layer of flour and her sink was piled with dishes.

For the second time that morning her doorbell rang. She couldn't remember ever being this popular. With Roark's warning ringing in her ear, she checked the peephole before she opened the door in case an ambitious reporter had tracked her down. Vance Waverly stood in her hallway.

She opened the door.

"Hel-l-o." Both his tone and his eyebrows rose as he took in her appearance.

Too late, Elizabeth realized if the kitchen was covered in flour, she probably was, as well. "What are you doing here?"

"Roark called me after you didn't pick up. He's worried about you."

"I'm fine."

"I can see that." He looked past her. "Doing a little baking?"

"A pumpkin pie."

"Then you're still planning on coming for Thanksgiving dinner?"

Was it that late already? She'd been so busy worrying about her sudden unemployment she had forgotten all about calling to cancel. "I really don't know if that's such a great idea. Sabeen was right. Roark and I aren't really engaged. You have to know he was only thinking of Waverly's."

"And you? What were you thinking about?" Vance set his

hand on the door frame and leaned in. "Why would a beautiful woman risk so much to help out a man she barely knew?"

"He's helping me." She waited for shock and outrage, but glimpsed only amusement. "What's so funny?"

"Roark could have had almost any woman in New York City, but he chose you. Have you asked yourself why?"

"No."

"You might want to."

The timer dinged on her stove, indicating that the pie was done and saving Elizabeth from having to reply. "Can I offer you some coffee?"

"Why don't I pour myself a cup while you get ready."

The words that would send him on his way hovered on her lips, but went unsaid. She really didn't want to be alone today.

"I have a lot of flour to wash off. It'll probably take me half an hour."

"The coffeepot looks full. I can wait."

"Afraid if you leave, I won't show up?"

"Of course not."

Elizabeth didn't believe him. Nor did she blame him for not trusting her. Facing even a small number of people today held little appeal.

An hour later, they arrived at Vance's palatial home in Forest Hills. Charlie's face reflected her relief as her husband escorted Elizabeth into the grand two-story foyer.

Despite the large scale of the rooms, Charlotte had managed to make the traditional styling welcoming and cozy. As Elizabeth slipped out of her coat, she couldn't help but compare the warm, elegantly decorated space to Roark's starkly appointed loft that, thanks to the odds and ends he'd collected on his travels, looked more like a Moroccan flea market than a home. The two living spaces were as different as the men who occupied them.

Vance, a wealthy businessman with a rock-solid personal life. Sophisticated and settled. His home, polished and perfect.

Roark, a scholar and an adventurer with a study crammed with books and a packed bag in his closet ready so he could be ready to leave town on a moment's notice. And then there was the penthouse on Fifth Avenue. Roark was a man holding on to his past because guilt kept him from confronting his mistakes and forgiving himself.

Envy ate at Elizabeth as she watched Vance kiss his wife and toss the toddler into the air. The room rang with the child's delighted cries and Elizabeth looked away. Not wishing to burden anyone with her melancholy, she moved apart and sat where she could gaze at the gardens behind the house.

She wanted what Charlie had. Wanted it so bad she couldn't breathe.

The strong, stable husband. The adorable toddler. The security of being loved and respected.

Instead, she'd fallen for yet another man who couldn't give her those things.

Would she ever learn?

Roark's flight from Cairo landed at JFK a little before four on Friday afternoon. He cleared customs without any trouble.

Brushing past the crowd shuffling toward baggage claim, he stretched his long legs and headed for the taxi area. He hoped the line wasn't long. Now that he'd landed in New York City, the need to see Elizabeth had gone from prickly urgency to gnawing compulsion.

A short, Middle Eastern man in a black suit caught up to him as he stepped into the icy November afternoon. "Mr. Black, I'm your driver."

Who'd sent a car for him? Vance knew his travel plans, but he'd never send a car.

"No, thanks. I'd rather catch a cab." To Roark's relief, only a handful of people stood in line ahead of him.

"But I have a car waiting."

After everything that transpired in Cairo, he was more cautious than ever about getting into a car with a stranger. If Masler had any idea that Roark was setting a trap for him, he would have sprung one of his own.

"Who sent you?" Roark demanded.

"I have instructions to bring you to Waverly's."

Not Masler then. It was probably Ann.

"No, thanks," Roark repeated. He had a driving need to see Elizabeth.

"But…"

Roark slammed the taxi door on the man's protests and gave the driver an address. His head fell back against the seat. His eyelids became heavy and he let them droop. He'd barely catnapped during the twelve-hour flight from Cairo. Normally he was able to sleep anywhere he considered safe. And what could be more secure than a plane flying at thirty-thousand feet? Today, however, he'd been pestered by regrets. Haunted by what Elizabeth had not said when he called to tell her he was heading out of town.

As exhausted as he was, Roark couldn't quite step across the threshold of sleep. He'd disappointed Elizabeth by running off on such short notice. She might not have asked, but she'd needed him to be there for her on Thanksgiving. He remembered how hard it had been to be alone with the news about his mother's death. Growing up, he'd never spent much time with kids his own age. Learning about friendship was something it had taken him years to figure out.

Even now, he could count on one hand the people he considered friends and most of those were buddies like Smith that he counted on when he needed help, not confidants he shared his aspirations and fears with.

In fact, until Elizabeth had entered his life, Vance was the only person Roark had confided in. And he'd never brought his half brother to his mother's apartment. Elizabeth alone had seen it and Roark remained baffled that he'd given her that glimpse into his psyche.

Gray and tan buildings swept past the taxi's window in a hypnotic blur as they neared the restaurant where Elizabeth was organizing a birthday party for one of her clients. She was in charge of setup. The restaurant would take care of the rest. Before he'd left for Cairo, the plan had been for him to pick her up at seven and take her out to dinner. He was here to make sure those plans hadn't changed.

Roark held the front door for two men carrying in an enormous cake decorated with realistic-looking women's shoes. Inside, the restaurant's urban edge had been softened with black tulle, strings of white lights and sprays of white ostrich feathers. Four-tops had been pushed together to make long rows and arranged in a horseshoe along the walls of the narrow restaurant. Down the center of the tables tall crystal candleholders alternated with crystal vases containing sprigs of greenery and white orchids. Roark saw Elizabeth in every detail.

A woman in her mid-thirties was showing two young women how the place settings needed to be set up. Elizabeth was nowhere in sight. He approached the trio.

"I'm looking for Elizabeth."

The woman in charge spoke. "You're Roark Black. I recognize your photo from Page Six." Her smile carried more than a trace of malice. "Elizabeth is no longer in charge of this event. Or any event for Josie Summers's Event Planning. She was fired." Her delight in Elizabeth's downfall was so obvious that Roark turned away without responding.

Without question, this had been his fault. Elizabeth was on her way to becoming Josie Summers's partner before he'd entered her life. Now, because Sabeen had behaved badly, Elizabeth had been terminated.

Flagging down another taxi, he headed for her apartment. She answered the door as if she'd been expecting his arrival. Her expression was neither surprised nor delighted and he half expected her to slam the door in his face. Instead, she stepped back, but made no welcoming gesture.

"Sabeen said you weren't returning to New York until Sunday." Her rebuke came through loud and clear.

Roark entered her apartment and dropped his duffel near the door. "Sabeen doesn't know my business."

"Neither does anyone else, apparently."

The black turtleneck she wore emphasized her skin's paleness. She'd fastened her long blond hair into a lackluster ponytail. She stood with her arms crossed over her chest, her shoulders hunched. This was not the vibrant woman he'd made love to on Wednesday morning.

"I went to the restaurant, but some woman said you'd been fired."

"Josie didn't think having one of her employees embroiled in a Page Six scandal was good for her business."

"We can fix this."

Instead of answering she retreated to her small dining table and picked up an envelope. "Here."

"What is this?"

"The money I took from you. It's all there."

He left his hands at his sides, letting her know he wasn't going to take the envelope. "I gave you the money in exchange for your help."

"What help? Thanks to Sabeen, everyone knows our engagement was fake. Your reputation is worse than before."

"It's her word against ours."

"It's more than that." She waggled the envelope to catch his attention. "I can't pretend anymore."

Her dejection wrenched at him. When she'd needed him to be at her side, he disappointed her. He didn't blame her for cutting her losses.

"Keep the money. This fiasco was my fault, not yours."

"I don't feel right taking it."

"How are you planning on paying for your next round of in vitro without it?"

She shoved her chin to a belligerent angle. "I'll manage."

"Don't be stubborn." He might have accepted her decision, if not for the dark circles beneath her eyes. It was his fault that she wasn't sleeping. That she'd lost her job. If he'd postponed his trip for a few days they could have confronted Sabeen's accusation together. She wouldn't have had to face the anniversary of her family's death alone. "Have you forgotten that you're out of a job?"

"Not likely."

Frustration rushed at him like a speeding bullet. "Why can't you just let me help you?"

"Because I don't feel right taking anything from you."

"Why not? I thought we were friends." Even as he said the words, he realized he thought of her as a lot more than that.

"Friends." She repeated the word too softly for Roark to catch any inflection that hinted at her thoughts.

Oh, who was he kidding? What he felt for her went way past friendship. But how far did it go? He instinctively shied away from the word *love*. He'd never shown a propensity for the commitment and responsibility to another required for that emotion.

And what could he expect from Elizabeth when he had no idea what he intended to offer her?

Bypassing the envelope she continued to hold out to him like some sort of shield, Roark stepped into her space and slid his fingers into the hair at the back of her head, undoing the ponytail. While her hair cascaded around her shoulders, he lowered his head and stole her surprised gasp.

After only a moment's hesitation, her lips moved beneath his, answering his passion with a hunger that sent his libido into overdrive. He crushed her body in his arms, plundered her mouth and drank from her moans.

When he'd planned how to get her to forgive him, storming her defenses with long, drugging kisses had been pretty far down his list. Her fingers burrowed beneath his shirt, finding skin. Any ability to think rationally vanished in a haze of desire so strong he tore buttons loose getting the shirt off. The shirt landed atop his leather jacket at his feet. A second later, he'd swept her into his arms and carried her the blessedly short distance to her bed.

With the mattress against her back she stiffened. "Wait."

Roark had already been waiting for days. His patience was long gone. Kissing his way down her neck, he traced his fingertip around the nipple that had hardened to a tight bud beneath the black silk camisole she wore. Her turtleneck lay on the floor beside his discarded clothes.

She arched her back, offering her body for his pleasure, but her next words blunted his desire. "Roark, stop. I'm angry with you."

He drifted his lips along the skin just above the camisole's lace edge, tantalizing her with kisses, but ventured no lower. If he wanted to make love to her, he could seduce her into forgetting everything that was wrong between them. But as the glow from their passionate reunion faded, the same issues would resurface. He'd abandoned her when she'd needed him. She wasn't going to forgive that easily.

"I'm sorry I took off the way I did."

"You're sorry?" She shoved at his chest until he rolled off her. Sitting up, she ran her fingers through her hair and glared at him. "Do you have any idea what I've been through in the last three days?"

"I have an idea."

"Sabeen humiliated me in front of your friends. Then my name was plastered all over Page Six in a career-ruining scandal. You asked why I gave you back your money. It's because I can't afford to have a child right now."

"I did this. Let me help you until you're back on your feet." She scrambled off the mattress. "I can't do this."

"Do what?"

"This." She waved her hand to indicate them both. "I never should have let you in today."

"Why did you?" Roark came to stand before her. He set his hands on her hips, slid his palm over the jut of her hipbone. Momentum carried him to the swell of her bottom.

"It's over between us," she said, ignoring his question.

He eased her against the thunderous ache in his groin, dropped his cheek to her soft golden hair. "It doesn't have to be."

"So I'm just supposed to be grateful you're going to stick around for the near future?" The edge in her tone told him the opposite would be true. "And then you go your way and I go mine?"

Silk sighed against his palm as he drew his hand up her spine. In seconds he could whisk the fabric over her head and bare her gorgeous breasts. The trembling in her limbs told him she was fighting what her body craved. Already the fists she'd made were loosening. The anger was ebbing out of her and with it, her determination to fight him.

"Can I borrow your shower?"

"I guess." The confusion in her bright blue eyes dominated the sensual fullness of her parted lips. She hadn't expected him to back off so easily and stood lost between battle and surrender.

"Thank you. It was a long flight from Cairo." He kissed her nose and headed for the bathroom.

She called after him. "Why aren't you showering at the loft?"

"Because your place is closer."

"Is that why you came over? To use my shower?"

Roark grinned as he turned on the water. The disappointment in Elizabeth's voice gave him hope. Naked, he stepped into the doorway and gave her an eyeful of what she'd just passed on.

"No, I came by to see you. I couldn't stop thinking about you the entire time I was gone."

Even if he lived an infinite number of lifetimes, he'd never stop enjoying the way she was staring at him at the moment. The stark lust in her eyes as her gaze drifted from his chest to his groin. The dreamy expression that told him she liked what she saw. And the way she bit down on her lower lip as if holding back was the most difficult thing she'd ever done.

"How was Cairo?" As if it took a great amount of will, she looked away. "Were you able to find Darius?"

"He was gone before I got there."

"What about the other thing you were looking for?"

"I got a lead."

He'd said the wrong thing.

"A lead." Her chest rose with the deep breath she sucked in. "When are you leaving again?"

"In a week or so." He stepped into the shower. She preferred a berry-scented body wash and shampoo. If he used it he would probably spend the rest of the day half aroused at the memory of her.

"What you're doing is dangerous, isn't it?" She'd stepped into the bathroom to pursue their conversation.

"There's an element of danger, but I take every precaution."

"This isn't what I signed up for." Her voice was closer. The door to the shower slid open. "Everything in my life was exactly the way I wanted it before you came along."

He snagged her wrist and drew her into the shower with him. She didn't protest. Not even when the water drenched her clothes.

"And it will get back to being that way again," he assured her, stripping the sodden fabric off her body.

"After you're gone?" She reached up on tiptoe and cupped his face in her hands. Her eyes were bottomless pools of angst as he gathered her in his arms.

"As soon as you take me up on my offer to start you in your own business and use the money I paid you to get pregnant."

"Thank you for reminding me what's most important in my life." And then she was kissing him, her tongue plunging into his mouth as passion ignited between them once again.

Eleven

Elizabeth shredded lettuce and watched Roark talk on the phone. It was 7:00 p.m. The lasagna she'd made earlier that day was due to come out of the oven in ten minutes. From the tone of Roark's voice and the annoyance pinching his mouth, she doubted he'd get a chance to sample her culinary skills.

"Can't this wait until Monday?" he demanded. From his duffel bag he'd pulled fresh clothes and a small bag containing toiletries. "I don't really give a damn what Ann wants." The rest of his side of the conversation was distorted when he headed into her bathroom.

Getting into that shower with him had been a mistake. The water might not have ruined her brand-new camisole, but she'd ruined any chance at a clean break with Roark. Despite spending the past two hours romping with him, hunger tugged at her loins. The lure of the man was her Achilles' heel.

"I've been summoned to Waverly's for a meeting with Ann Richardson. Supposedly there's some huge crisis that can't wait until Monday morning." He wrapped his arms around her waist and kissed her cheek. "I can be back in an hour."

"I don't think you should come back." The words took all her courage to say.

"What's wrong? I thought we straightened everything out."

"I know. I'm sorry if my behavior was misleading." She kept her cheek pressed tight to his chest. If she looked into his eyes, she would never get the words out. "I can't keep seeing you. Every time you walk away I wonder if it's the last time we'll be together. Living on the edge of the unknown is what makes you happy. It's tearing me apart."

"Elizabeth."

The throb in his voice put a lump in her throat the size of a golf ball. Talking was impossible so she whispered. "Please understand how hard this is for me."

"It doesn't have to be hard. You've become important to me."

This was a powerful admission coming from Roark. Elizabeth listened to his steady heartbeat and fought to stay strong. "You've become important to me, too. That's why I need to stop seeing you. Before it hurts too much."

That was a lie. It already hurt too much. She'd been blindsided when she'd heard that her sister and her family were dead. The pain had been instant and devastating. Losing Roark was like slowly being smothered beneath a pile of stones. The ache was crushing the life from her with each second that ticked by.

"I don't want to lose you." Roark took her face in his hands and searched her eyes.

She scrutinized him in return, but he'd closed off all emotion. "Please don't ask me to be your friend." She tried to smile, but couldn't compel her facial muscles to produce an emotion she wasn't feeling. "There'd always be this sexual energy between us that I'd give in to. We'd hook up. In a day or a week, you'd disappear and I'd be left resenting you because you'll never be happy settling down in New York."

"You've got it all figured out, don't you?"

"I know my pattern. It's why I'd decided to have a baby on my own. I'm always falling for the wrong sort of guy."

"Like me."

"Like you."

Roark would never be domesticated. He had no interest in being part of a traditional family. As a child he'd spent too much time alone. He'd learned about independence, not what it meant to rely on someone. While his brother was content to be a husband and a father, Roark craved adventure. It wasn't fair to be frustrated with him because she expected too much. But she didn't have to bang her head against a wall either.

"So, if I really care about you, I should leave you alone."

No. If you really care about me, you should stay in New York and spend the rest of your life making me the happiest woman on earth.

"Yes, you should leave me alone."

Heart breaking, she continued, "The reason for us being together no longer exists."

"Then I'll stay away." He grazed her forehead with his lips, picked up his jacket and duffel and headed toward her front door.

Was she making a mistake? He said he didn't want to lose her, but she'd not given him a chance to tell her where he wanted to take their relationship. She just assumed it wasn't where she wanted to go. And yet by abandoning her at Thanksgiving when he knew how devastating the holiday would be for her, he'd demonstrated exactly where his priorities lay.

The guessing game tore at her confidence and reminded her how many times she'd played this same game with herself.

"Roark…"

He'd reached the hallway and turned when she spoke his name. His face was granite, but behind in his eyes intense emotions burned. "I would only end up hurting you. I never wanted that. You have to do what's right for you. Goodbye, Elizabeth."

She should be grateful that he was sympathetic to her plight and strong enough to follow through when she would have called him back and repeated her mistakes. But she couldn't feel happy or even relieved that their relationship had ended cleanly. After such a short time together, her heart should be barely bruised.

So, why did her chest ache and her eyes burn with unshed tears?

Because she'd fallen in love him despite all her determination to be smarter this time. And that made her a first-class idiot because his actions had demonstrated that she would always come a distant second to his adventures.

Roark caught a taxi in front of Elizabeth's apartment and directed it to Waverly's. This wasn't how he'd expected his day to end. The lasagna cooking in Elizabeth's oven made his mouth water and he realized it had been over twelve hours since he'd eaten anything. Food hadn't seemed important while he was gorging himself on sensual delicacies. With Elizabeth in his arms, nothing else mattered.

So, why had he let her push him away? His instincts demanded that he stay and fight for her. Walking out her door had been one of the hardest things he'd ever done. If not for his decision he'd made after his mother's death to avoid all romantic entanglements, he might have…

What?

She wanted something from him he couldn't commit to. A family. Security. He wasn't cut out to settle down and be someone's everything. Hadn't he failed his mother? Wasn't his leaving what had made her heart give out? He swore he'd never get close enough to hurt anyone like that again.

The taxi let Roark out in front of Waverly's. This late on a Friday, all of the building's seven floors were dark except the top one where Waverly's executives ran the business. He paused before approaching the building. When Vance had first brought him into the Waverly's fold, Roark had been adamant in his refusal to be tied to an office and a day-to-day routine. But after spending three months in the Amazon, eluding thugs with machine guns, and the troubles over the Gold Heart statue, he no longer perceived Waverly's as a straightjacket he needed to avoid.

Kendra Darling pushed open the front door as he neared. She reminded him of Elizabeth. A career woman hiding her femininity behind tortoise-shell glasses, unglamorous pantsuits and professionalism.

"You're working late," he remarked, passing from the chilly November night into the impressive foyer.

An enormous crystal chandelier cast a soft glow over the classical artwork adorning polished-wood paneling. During the day Waverly's clients strode along the gold carpet or sat on one of the couches upholstered in rich fabrics that dotted the large space. Tonight, the empty space had a haunted quality.

"I'm supposed to escort you up as soon as you arrive." As Ann's longtime assistant, Kendra was used to dealing with all sorts of tough situations, from unhappy clients to nosy reporters.

"Ann doesn't think I can find my own way?"

"After you refused the car I sent to pick you up, she insisted I make sure you weren't sidetracked."

"Lead the way."

Ann wasn't behind her desk when Kendra gestured him into the CEO's office. Roark could tell by Ann's agitated pacing as she wore a path from one tall, narrow window to the next that something was seriously wrong.

"Where have you been?"

Great. She was on fire. "Cairo."

"How dare you take off without telling me."

"I had something I needed to take care of."

"Do you know what's happened?"

"Fill me in."

"His Highness Raif Khouri called. His uncle, Mallik, was left at the altar by his young royal bride."

At first relief blasted through him that Darius had succeeded in freeing the woman he loved from her intended's villainous plot. Annoyance arrived a moment later. If Roark's connection to this event came to light, it might prove the final nail in the coffin for Waverly's.

"What does that have to do with me?"

"He's blaming all the trouble on the curse that has befallen his family because the Gold Heart statue is missing from the palace."

"His uncle's troubles have nothing to do with their missing statue."

"I know that, but Raif is adamant that we produce our statue. He's convinced it is the one stolen from the palace."

"It isn't."

"Then produce it so we can prove that."

"I can't."

"Why not?"

"Because the Gold Heart statue's provenance documents are missing and until I can get them back from the man who stole them, the prince could claim that it's his and we'd have no proof it wasn't."

Ann gasped. "He'd never do that."

"Maybe not, but I'm the one the FBI believes stole the statue."

"The reputation of Waverly's is resting on that statue." Ann's voice throbbed with anger and worry.

"You don't think I know that?"

"I need that statue. I'm flying to Rayas next Thursday to meet with His Highness and he's expecting me to produce the statue. Without it we'll be ruined."

"I'm working on getting the documents back, but it's not going to happen by next Thursday."

Leaving Ann seething with annoyance, Roark passed by Vance's office on his way back to the elevator and wasn't surprised to find it dark. Since Charlie had come into his life, Vance's priorities had shifted. He now put family before business and seemed happy with the new arrangement.

Was it really that simple?

Roark jabbed the down button on the elevator. He rolled his shoulders to ease the tension, but relief wasn't in his future. Too much was wrong in his life at the moment.

Unless he retrieved the missing provenance documents, he had no way of proving that the Gold Heart statue owned by Sheikh Rashid bin Mansour was not the one missing from Rayas's palace.

Then there was Darius, who'd stolen a royal bride from Mallik Khouri and was on the run.

And worst of all, he'd lost the one bright spot in this whole misadventure. Elizabeth. She'd sent him packing, and he had no idea how to change her mind. Nor was he sure he should even try. She deserved to be happy and if being with him made her miserable, he should put her feelings first and let her be. Unfortunately, every fiber of his being rejected that as the worst idea he'd ever had.

As he was leaving Waverly's, his phone rang. It was Smith.

"Got them," the former marine said.

Relief rushed through Roark. "They okay?"

"Fine." Behind Smith were the sounds of laughter and conversation. "We'll be in New York by tomorrow."

"Bring them to the loft. They can stay here until we can make sure Fadira is safe from her father and Khouri."

Roark caught a cab and headed to the apartment Darius and Sabeen shared. She would be anxious for word about her brother and Roark wanted to talk to her about what she'd done to Elizabeth.

"Your brother and Fadira are safe and heading to New York," Roark said when Sabeen opened the door.

With a cry she hugged him. "I've been so worried."

And Roark could see that she had been. All at once she was the happy young girl she'd been before her father's death.

"Let's have a drink and celebrate." She caught Roark's hand and led him toward the couch.

"I can't stay."

"One drink," she cajoled.

Roark twisted free of her grip and crossed his arms over his chest.

She pouted. "What's wrong?"

"You ask that, after what you did to Elizabeth at the gala?"

Defiance flared in her eyes. "You're angry because everyone knows you aren't engaged?"

"I asked you to keep quiet about what you knew, not broadcast my business to the media. Elizabeth has lost her job. Waverly's is in more trouble than ever. What were you thinking?"

"That if she was out of your life you would see that I'm all the woman you'll ever need."

"That's your excuse? You were jealous of a woman I was pretending to be engaged to?" He downplayed his deeper feelings for Elizabeth to give his reprimand more punch.

"She might be pretending, but you are not." Sabeen rushed at the desk and placed both palms on its surface. "I see how you look at her. You're in love with her, and she doesn't feel the same way."

Sabeen's accusation smacked into his diaphragm. "You don't know what you're talking about," he told her.

"You don't think I know when a woman's in love? She feels it here." With a dramatic flourish, Sabeen covered her heart with her right hand. "And it shows here." She gestured to her eyes.

Pain bloomed in Roark's head. Was Sabeen right about Elizabeth? If she loved him wouldn't she want him in his life? His thoughts retreated to his afternoon with Elizabeth. He'd glimpsed something in her gaze as he'd made love to her, but had he mistaken passion for love?

And what did it matter anyway? She'd made her feelings clear. Their relationship was over. She would have her baby. He would return to hunting antiquities. They'd enjoyed a few delightful weeks. Made memories he could reflect on the next time he got stuck in the jungle for months on end.

"Look in my eyes," Sabeen continued. She cupped his head and met his gaze. "See how I burn for you."

Roark did look, but all he saw was insecurity. Sabeen had latched on to him as a lifeline after her father's death. At the time she'd been young and frightened by the loss of a second parent in six years. Today, she was no longer a child, but a capable woman with the ability to take care of herself. Time she discovered that.

"I'm taking away your allowance until you prove to me you're ready to accept responsibility for your inheritance. This week's stunt demonstrates that you are a child in a woman's body. Everything has come easily for you and you've not matured because of it."

She obviously wasn't expecting this. Her nostrils flared. "I am a woman. A woman who loves you."

"A child who loves me. Like an older brother." Clarity startled him with its sudden appearance. "That's it, isn't it? Darius has won his princess and plans to marry her. You're afraid that

Elizabeth will take me away from you. That's why you sabotaged her. You're afraid to be alone."

A fat tear rolled down Sabeen's cheek, but her eyes remained confrontational. "I hate you." She pushed away from his chair and raced out of the room.

Feeling much older than his twenty-seven years, Roark left the apartment, but didn't feel much like heading back to his empty loft.

Forty minutes later he let himself into his mother's apartment. He'd called ahead to let Mrs. Myott know he was coming. She had leftover pot roast waiting for him. Seated at the center island, he wolfed down the meal. She'd slow-cooked the meat and it practically melted in his mouth.

Mrs. Myott drank coffee and watched him over the rim of her cup. "When did you last eat?"

"On the plane. It's been a hectic few hours since I landed."

"Here's the envelope that came for you today." She slid a plain manila envelope toward him.

Roark set down his fork and picked up the envelope. It bore his name and nothing more. Curious, he slit open the flap with his knife and pulled out a smaller envelope bearing his mother's bold handwriting.

She'd addressed the envelope to Edward Waverly.

"Who sent this?"

"I don't know. I received a call from the doorman that he'd received an envelope addressed to you."

"Did he say which courier service dropped it off?"

"It never occurred to me to ask." Mrs. Myott had also recognized the familiar handwriting. Sadness darkened her eyes. "Why would someone send you a letter your mother wrote to Edward Waverly?"

"I have no idea." Roark suspected she told Edward she was pregnant and never received a reply. If he'd wanted nothing to do with an illegitimate son, why then had he written a letter to Vance telling him about his half brother so many years later?

Hoping for a clue as to who sent his mother's letter, Roark

peered into the envelope and spied a sheet of paper. He pulled it out. An unfamiliar hand had penned a short note.

Your mother wrote this letter to Edward Waverly. You are as much a Waverly as Vance.

Vance was the only person Roark could imagine having access to Edward Waverly's personal correspondence, but he knew Vance's handwriting and this wasn't it. Mystified, he handed Mrs. Myott the note and then carefully pulled a sheet of yellowed paper from the envelope.

To My Love,

I have kept a secret from you all these years and done you a terrible wrong. You have a son. Roark turned eighteen yesterday and enlisted in the marines. I have never been so proud of him, nor so filled with regret. I know now that by holding him too tight all these years, I instead drove him away.

I'm sorry I didn't tell you the truth sooner. When you left me I was devastated. It took months for me to accept that I mustn't blame you for moving forward with your life. I could never have been the wife you needed. The world outside these walls is too big and too terrifying for me to face. In the end, my fears were stronger than my love for you.

Many nights I paced the floor, debating whether or not to tell you about Roark. In the end, I was afraid that if you knew you had a son you would take him into the world and away from me. I couldn't bear to lose both of the men that I loved. Please don't take your anger with me out on Roark. From a stubborn and clever boy he has grown into a determined and intelligent man. You will be proud to claim him as your son.

Forever yours,

Guinevere

Here was the admission from his mother Roark had been waiting all his life for. He stared at his mother's letter. Strange how he felt no different now than he had a moment ago. No lights came on in his mind. Nothing snapped into place. The words left him numb.

He didn't even care that Edward Waverly had never sought him out after discovering the truth. What good would it do to resent a man who'd been dead almost five years? His parents' relationship was complicated and colored by bitterness. It was their difficulties that had kept them apart his entire life. Nothing at all to do with him. And in a strange way, Roark was glad he and Vance had been able to begin their relationship free of their father's baggage.

Then, slowly he became aware that one change had happened. Reading his mother's letter had dispelled the restlessness that drove him to spend his days seeking his place in the world. He knew where he belonged. Who he was. The hazy doubts he'd always carried in the back of his mind about being Vance's half brother were a thing of the past. He was a Waverly. In blood if not name. Waverly's wasn't a straightjacket to be avoided at all costs, but his family's legacy and he was going to do whatever it took to save it from the likes of Dalton Rothschild.

"Roark, are you all right?" Mrs. Myott had come to stand beside him. Her hand covered his.

He blinked and reoriented himself in the penthouse. The hum of the refrigerator. The lingering scent of the pot roast. The comforting sight of Mrs. Myott's face. "I'm fine. Just need to make a phone call."

Even though he wasn't sure if she'd pick up, Roark dialed Elizabeth's number. To his relief, she answered.

"Roark?"

"Someone delivered a ten-year-old letter to the penthouse from my mother to Edward Waverly telling him about me."

"Who?"

"It was delivered by messenger. I have no idea where it came from."

"Vance?"

"Not his handwriting and definitely not his style."

"How odd." Her voice took on a thoughtful note. "And after all this time. Do you think it was recently discovered?"

"Edward has been dead five years. Vance went through all his papers. That's where he found the letter telling him about me. I know if he'd found this letter he would have given it to me immediately."

"So why has it surfaced now?"

"Because Waverly's is in more trouble than ever. The note that accompanied the letter states that I'm as much a Waverly as Vance. The auction house is as much my responsibility to save as Vance's."

"So, what are you going to do?"

"Fight."

"How? With George Cromwell stepping down, there's no one to stop Rothschild from securing the votes he needs from the Waverly's board."

"It might help if I had someone by my side to help me."

"You have Vance and Ann."

"I was thinking about you."

"Me?" Her tone sharpened. "I can't help you, Roark. Even if we could somehow make the world believe our engagement wasn't a lie, you aren't going to stick around as long as it's going to take to save Waverly's. It's not in your nature."

"What if my nature has changed?"

"I don't believe it can any more than I believe you want it to." She spoke so softly it was hard to hear her words. "Maybe it's time to give up on Waverly's. Let Rothschild have it. Ann's brilliant, she'll land on her feet. Vance has numerous businesses to occupy him."

"And the hundreds of people Waverly's employs? What of them?"

Elizabeth didn't speak for a long time. Roark tamped down his frustration. Had he really expected her to come running just because he'd received a letter confirming he was a Waverly? She'd never truly believed he was committed to saving Waverly's. And he'd further damaged her trust when he'd run off to Egypt the day before Thanksgiving.

"I'm sorry, I can't help you, Roark. I really do hope you can save Waverly's. It sounds like you're fully committed to the task."

"I appreciate your faith in me. Good night, Elizabeth."

"Goodbye, Roark."

He didn't miss the finality of her words as the phone went dead in his hand.

Twelve

The Monday after Thanksgiving dawned with clear skies and temperatures in the forties. All dressed up, but with no place she had to be, Elizabeth headed to the coffee shop on the corner. She had to get out of her apartment and at least pretend she was making progress. After spending Sunday updating her résumé and assembling a digital portfolio of her best work, she'd emailed all of Josie's competitors, praying one of them would give her a shot. The holiday season took its toll on event planners. Surely someone could use an extra set of hands.

For an hour she sipped coffee and stared out the window. On her laptop awaited the phone numbers she would dial. Nerves kept the coffee from sitting well in her stomach. What if she couldn't find a job doing what she was good at? How was she supposed to start over?

Five phone calls later, anxiety had turned to dread. A stone had lodged itself in her throat making talking difficult. It wasn't just that no one had an opening or was unimpressed with her work. Three of the five event planners warned her that Josie planned to wage war on anyone who hired her.

She was sunk.

Her phone rang. Elizabeth checked the unfamiliar number against the companies she'd sent résumés to. It matched none of them. She hit Talk.

"Elizabeth Minerva?"

"Yes."

"Please hold for Mrs. Fremont."

Her heart thumped against her ribs like a loose shutter in a hurricane. Sonya Fremont was calling her?

"Elizabeth. You were supposed to call me if ever you got free of that employer of yours."

"I know. I just assumed that with the Page Six article…" She let her words trail off. What if Sonya didn't read the gossip page? Had Elizabeth just blown any chance of working with the woman? And what if she got the job and was later fired because Sonya found out about the whole fake engagement with Roark?

"Oh, for heaven's sakes, Elizabeth. This is New York City. You're already yesterday's news."

"I am?"

Sonya laughed. "I've never heard anybody sound so glad to have their fifteen minutes of fame behind them."

Elizabeth's confidence was returning with each second. "I think you'll find I'm happier behind the scenes."

"And that's what I'd like to talk to you about. Now that you're no longer employed by that woman, I'd like to hire you to plan the gala. Your proposal was original and inspiring. Can you come by tomorrow to discuss a few minor changes I'd like to make?"

"Of course."

Did this mean she was going into business for herself? Josie's decision to blackball her from working with other event planners had backed Elizabeth into a corner. Hope floated through her, erasing most of her doubts.

After she hung up with Sonya, Elizabeth tackled a list of things she'd need to go into business for herself. The money she'd tried to return to Roark would have to be diverted from her fertility treatments to rent, food and other basic survival needs. Was it enough to last until she could find other clients?

Elizabeth dialed the fertility clinic. She needed to cancel her upcoming appointments. She'd already come to terms with the reality that motherhood would have to wait until she could afford it. The switchboard connected her to Bridget Sullivan, her doctor's nurse. In the eight months Elizabeth had been trying to get pregnant, Bridget had been so kind to her. She deserved an explanation why Elizabeth couldn't move forward at the moment.

"I just wanted to let you know that I've cancelled my upcoming appointments."

"Of course you have," Bridget crowed. "Congratulations."

This was so far from the sympathetic response she'd braced for that Elizabeth wondered if Bridget knew who was on the phone. "Bridget, this is Elizabeth Minerva."

"What timing. I have your file in front of me. I was about to give you a call."

"But you said congratulations."

Now it was Bridget's turn to be confused. "I thought you'd be thrilled. You're pregnant. Isn't that what you've been hoping for all these months?"

"Pregnant? How is that possible?"

Bridget laughed. "Since I'm confident you haven't been cheating on us with another fertility clinic, I'm guessing that fiancé of yours has the right stuff. You must be over the moon. A baby on the way and a wedding to plan. You're one lucky lady."

"Lucky." It wasn't the first word that she'd use to describe her current situation. She was pregnant? The room tilted as she tried to absorb what she'd just heard. "But two rounds of in vitro failed. Dr. Abbot told me it would be impossible for me to get pregnant without help."

"I don't know how to explain it other than sometimes miracles happen. A couple that has struggled with fertility for years adopts a child and suddenly the wife is pregnant. Maybe you just needed to find the right guy."

But Roark wasn't the right guy for her. He was an amazing

man. A terrific lover. Wonderful friend. Loyal to the core, but he wasn't interested in making a commitment to her or anyone.

"Do you need us to recommend an obstetrician? I can email you a list."

"That would be great." Her thoughts were like cotton in her head. Thanking Bridget, she disconnected the call and stared at the list of event planners on her laptop screen.

In the space of ten minutes she'd become an entrepreneur and learned she was pregnant. What if she wasn't ready to tackle both at the same time?

And Roark. How angry would he be when she told him he was going to be a father? This was all her fault. She'd told him she couldn't get pregnant. He would think she'd tricked him.

Elizabeth caught a cab and gave the driver the address for Roark's loft. In the back of her mind, she knew it would be prudent to call ahead and warn him she was coming, but after breaking things off, what was she supposed to give him as an excuse for needing to see him? Telling him that she was pregnant with his child was not a conversation she wanted to have on the phone.

She rapped on Roark's door. The sound barely drowned out the thunder of her heart as she anticipated the scene to come. Conversation openers spun through her head while she waited, making her dizzy. Her nerve was fading by the second. She'd actually started backing down the hall when Roark's door opened. A beautiful young woman with disheveled dark hair peered out. She wore a sleepy expression and a gorgeous turquoise silk nightgown that hinted at the flawless figure beneath.

"Hello?" She spoke in accented English. "Can I help you?"

This was yet another development Elizabeth hadn't foreseen. Her first impulse was to make an excuse and race away, but she'd never been one to run from her problems. "I'm looking for Roark."

"He's not here." Her dark brown eyes smiled. "Are you a friend?"

"Yes." Elizabeth's head bobbed. "Elizabeth Minerva."

"I am Fadira. How wonderful to meet you."

This was the woman Darius had raced halfway around the

world to save. Elizabeth understood his fascination. Fadira was breathtaking.

"Do you know where Roark might have gone?"

"I do not, but he may have called while I was sleeping. Please come in." The woman opened the door wide and turned to address someone inside the loft. "Darling, have you heard from Roark this morning?"

Darius appeared beside the slim Middle Eastern woman and put his arm around her waist. She leaned into his embrace and slid her hand onto his bare chest.

"Hello, Elizabeth. I see you have met my fiancée."

Tears sprang to her eyes. "Congratulations."

"She is looking for Roark," Fadira explained.

"I thought he might be here." Renewed anxiety displaced her momentary relief. "I'm sorry to intrude. I should have called before coming over."

"Roark didn't tell you that he gave us the apartment for a few days?" Darius asked. "I have not heard from him since he left Saturday night. Are you worried about him?"

"Nothing like that. I had something I wanted to discuss with him. Do you know where he might have gone?"

"No. I'm sorry."

Which meant her news would have to wait a little while longer.

Roark sat at the desk in his mother's bedroom and for the first time, read the entries she'd made after he'd left for the marines. It had taken him two days of wandering like a ghost through the penthouse before he been able to face his mother's heartache.

He'd spent those days reliving memories of her. How he'd done his homework at this desk, while she'd sat in her favorite chair by the fireplace and read. If he'd gotten stuck on a math problem or wanted to discuss a social studies assignment, she was always close, ready to offer what help she could. Sometimes he pretended he didn't understand just so she'd lean over his shoulder. Her light, floral scent would fill his nostrils while her musical voice would explain the complexities of iambic pentameter or point out where he'd gone wrong with a formula.

To his surprise, his mother hadn't been devastated by his departure. She'd been proud that he'd chosen to serve his country, and she'd understood that he needed to make his mark on the world.

If he'd had the courage to say goodbye, he wouldn't have been burdened by guilt all these years. He could have left knowing that his mother wished nothing but the best for him.

Instead he'd acted like a fool and his mother had suffered. He'd hurt her like he'd hurt Elizabeth. All because he believed that love was a trap he had to avoid at all costs. An obligation that interfered with his freedom.

Well, Elizabeth hadn't tried to hold on to him and these past few days without her had been some of the most miserable hours of his life.

"Roark?" Elizabeth's soft voice came from the doorway. "I hope it's okay that Mrs. Myott let me in."

Dressed in a dark gray wool coat, her cheeks pink from the cold, she stood just outside the room as if afraid of her welcome.

His heart soared at the sight of her. "It's fine." More than fine. It was fantastic. Since she'd turned him down a second time on Friday night, he'd been moldering in a stew of recrimination. Unable to contain his relief, he crossed the room and hauled her into his arms, whirling her off her feet. "How'd you know to find me here?"

For two complete spins she melted into his embrace and he savored the peace he always felt in her company. The second her toes met the floor once again, she pushed out of his arms.

"I stopped by the loft." She moved out of reach. "Darius said he hadn't heard from you since Saturday. I couldn't think of anyplace else you might have gone." She gazed around the room, not meeting his eyes. "I met Fadira. I'm so glad they're able to be together."

"They blamed the canceled wedding on the missing statue," Roark said. "Which of course means that the Rayas royal family is more determined than ever to get their hands on the Gold

Heart statue Waverly's is going to auction. Ann needs me to give her the statue I found, but I still haven't located the missing documentation."

"What are you going to do?"

"Stall Ann and get the documents back. I've got a lead on them. The man who stole them has business in the Bahamas in a week. I plan on heading down there to get them back."

"How do you know he'll have them?"

"I had a chat with an acquaintance of his in Cairo."

"What sort of a chat?"

"The sort that gets information."

"And after you get the documents back, what then?"

"Waverly's reputation is saved. The Gold Heart statue is brought up for auction. We fight off whatever Dalton Rothschild has in store for us next."

She seemed to have run out of questions. That was fine. He had a few of his own.

"Would you come with me?"

"Where?"

"For starters to the Bahamas. You no longer have work as an excuse to stay in New York."

"I can't just go."

"Why not? You have nothing keeping you here."

"It's my home."

"I'm not asking you to move across the world, just to spend a couple weeks seeing new places, meeting new people."

"What happens when a couple weeks becomes a month, then six months? What if I get to a point where I never want to leave you?"

"Then don't." He snatched her back into his arms and tasted her surprise as his mouth settled on hers. She met the searching plunge of his tongue with a joyful moan and slid her fingers into his hair.

In an instant everything that had been dull in his world burst into vivid color. Kissing her was like the return of spring after a long cold winter. She was sunshine and warming earth, lilac and hyacinth. Nothing in the world compared to having her in his arms.

"Roark." Her breath came in soft pants. "I have something I need to tell you."

He'd surrendered her mouth so that he could nibble his way down her neck. She arched her back, pressing her breasts into his chest. Her coat was on the floor at her feet. In a few minutes he intended for her black suit to join it.

His fingers plucked her white blouse free of her pants. "I'm all ears."

"No, you're not," she gasped, grabbing for his hands a second too late. He'd released the clasp on her bra and swallowed one breast in his palm. "You're all hands."

"And lips." His mouth covered hers.

Slow and deep, he kissed her until all resistance vanished. He scooped her up and sat down in his mother's favorite chair with Elizabeth cradled in his lap.

"You're going to want to stop once you hear what I have to say," she warned him, her fingers fanned across his cheek. She brushed his lower lip with her thumb.

"Nothing you could say would ever make me want to stop making love to you," he told her.

Here in his mother's bedroom, surrounded by her things, he'd discovered something. He was no longer the boy who'd run away to join the marines because he needed adventure. He was the man who had found the adventure of a lifetime in the woman he held in his arms.

"Oh, I think this one will." She drew her finger between his brows, exploring the frown her words had produced. "What's the one thing you dread more than anything else in the world?"

"Until four days ago, I would have said being tied down to a place and responsible for another person's happiness."

She nodded sagely. "I'm pregnant."

Joy hit him square in the chest. "Congratulations."

"Congratulations?" She gaped at him, so obviously expecting him to be horrified because she was pregnant with his child.

"Well, yes." He cocked his head and searched her expression. "Isn't that what you wanted?"

The heel of her hand collided with his chest and she levered herself off his lap. "It's what *I* wanted. Not what *you* wanted."

"I want you to be happy." And all he'd done lately was upset her. "You are happy, aren't you?"

"How can an intelligent man like you be so dense?"

Easily, the blood had evacuated his brain and settled in his groin. Even now with her indigo eyes flashing danger signals at him and her unconfined breasts moving with distracting enticement beneath her blouse, his craving for her increased.

"Come sit down." He patted his thighs. "And I'll explain it to you."

Her eyes widened as her gaze trailed up his thighs and found him fully aroused. Her cheek color deepened, but when he held out his hand to her, she backed up.

"You aren't listening." She pointed at her stomach. "You're going to be a father."

His entire life he'd dreaded those six words. And now that he'd heard them? Now that the six words had turned his world upside down? The freedom he cherished: in jeopardy. The career he lived for: too dangerous. The woman he loved: bound to him forever. Life had never been more perfect.

She hadn't moved far enough away to escape his reach. All Roark had to do was lean forward and catch her wrist. Before the gasp passed her lips she was back on his lap, imprisoned by his arms.

Roark eyed her solemnly. "Are you okay about this?"

"Am I okay?" She stared at him as if he'd lost his mind. "Are you okay?"

"Very okay."

Before he could demonstrate exactly how okay he was, she stopped his lips from reaching hers by turning her head. "You have to know I don't expect anything from you."

"Oh, surely you have some expectations." He seized her earlobe between his teeth to distract her from the fact that he was steadily unbuttoning her blouse.

She shook her head. "I planned from the start to be a single mom. Nothing has changed."

"You have no job." The last button gave way. Pushing the edges of her blouse aside, he spanned her flat stomach with his hand and marveled at the life growing beneath. "No money."

"Sonya Fremont offered me the gala." She covered his hand with hers. "Other projects will come up."

"And how will you live in the meantime?"

"I'll do kids' birthday parties." She grimaced. "Weddings if I have to. Whatever it takes."

"And run yourself ragged in the process. You have more than yourself to worry about now. There's the baby to consider."

She scowled at him. "You don't think I know that?"

"Have you thought about what's going to happen after the baby's born? Are you going to take time off? Your apartment is barely big enough for you. What happens when the baby comes along?"

"Everything will work out fine." Her eyes glinted with confidence. "I'm not worried."

"Well, I am. For the last two days I've been sitting in this empty apartment, thinking about your situation and remembering how it once was filled with laughter and love. It's a waste of real estate, don't you think?"

"I guess." She caught her lip between her teeth and eyed him from beneath her long lashes. "Are you thinking it's time to sell?"

"I promised Mrs. Myott I wouldn't do that."

"So, what are you going to do with it?"

"I thought maybe you'd like to live here."

Her jaw dropped. "I couldn't. This place is too much. You don't even live here."

"Maybe that's something else that needs to change."

"You said you could never live here. That all the memories of your mother reminded you why she died."

"Maybe it's time some new memories were made here. Memories that wouldn't replace the ones I have of my mother, but that would blunt the guilt I feel for how I left."

She threw her arms around his neck and hugged him hard. "I think that's a wonderful idea."

Had she figured out what he'd just offered her? Roark hadn't meant to present his proposal in such a roundabout fashion, but teasing Elizabeth was something he enjoyed.

"Then you'll live here with me?"

"With you?" She leaned back and gazed at him in confusion. "But you're not staying in New York."

"As soon as I've cleaned up the situation with the Gold Heart statue, that's exactly what I intend to do."

She narrowed her eyes. "For how long?"

"For however long you want me."

"Do you mean that?" She sounded breathless. Unsure.

"When I headed to Cairo on Wednesday, it was the first time I didn't want to leave New York. And the entire time I was gone, I was miserable. All because of you."

"You missed me?" Hope sparked in her eyes. Roark was glad to be the one who put it there.

"Terribly."

"I'm really glad you want to be a part of your child's life."

"More than just a part of it." Roark watched her smile fade as his statement sank in. "Marry me and I swear I'll be there for you and our children as long as I live."

"Oh, Roark. That's the most perfect thing anyone has ever said to me." She hugged him hard and kissed him softly. Her tears dampened his cheeks. "But I can't ask you to do that. You're an adventurer. Seeking artifacts, finding treasure no one has seen for hundreds of years, that's your passion. It's what makes you happy."

"You make me happy. The rest is stuff I did while waiting for you to come into my life and make me complete."

"I love you," she told him, her voice fierce. Her joy was the most beautiful thing he'd ever seen. "I didn't realize how empty my life was until you came along. I guess what I needed was a little adventure." She kissed him sweetly on the lips. "Are you sure you won't miss all the excitement of chasing artifacts and tangling with bad guys?"

Roark chuckled as he recalled those three miserable months he'd spent in the Amazon. "Lately I've discovered that living on the edge has lost its appeal. I will continue to do the research and let others take all the risks." It was time to tackle a whole new set of challenges. "From now on, you and our baby are all the excitement I need."

Thirteen

Elizabeth leaned against the veranda railing, her attention riveted on the gorgeous male emerging from the azure water. Morning sunlight sparkled off his wet torso, highlighting the chiseled perfection of his abs and dazzling her already overstimulated hormones. This was their third morning on the island. The third time she'd enjoyed the spectacle of her magnificent husband returning to her from the sea.

"The water is wonderful," he announced, mounting the steps to the porch that surrounded their quaint beach cottage. "Why don't you join me?"

"And miss the view?"

"It's better close up." He hooked his arm around her waist and pulled her against his wet body.

Heedless of the damage the saltwater was doing to her silk nightgown, Elizabeth lifted on tiptoe and brushed her lips against his. "So it is."

Being married to Roark had far exceeded her expectations. From the second he'd found out she was carrying his child, the walls he'd erected around his heart had tumbled down. No shadows darkened his gray-green eyes. His smiles had become broader, less lopsided. He made love to her with the same single-minded passion, but the reverence in his caresses brought tears to her eyes.

Following the pattern of the past three mornings, Elizabeth joined Roark in the shower. As her hands stroked over his soap-slick body, she reveled in the joy of her fortune. What if her moratorium against bad boys had led her to refuse to act as Roark's fiancée? She never would have had the chance to discover that there was so much more to him than he let the world see.

With Roark sated by their second passionate encounter of the morning, Elizabeth knew this was the best time to approach him about yesterday's unsettled argument. While he lay sprawled on his back in the middle of the bed, she lifted his phone off the nightstand and rolled back toward him. His eyes were closed, but the corners of his lips drifted upward as her breasts made contact with his chest.

"You've got to call Ann and tell her what you're up to."

His palm coasted over her naked butt and up her spine in a possessive caress. "I really don't think she'll want to hear how I've spent my last three days."

Elizabeth ignored the delight tickling over her skin and forced herself to be firm. "Call her back. She's left three messages."

Roark opened one eye. "How do you know that?"

"I might have spoken with Kendra about the pre-auction exhibit for the Gold Heart collection."

He exhaled harshly. "We both agreed no Waverly's trouble, Gold Heart statue, or event planning emergencies while we're on our honeymoon."

"I know what I promised, but I haven't been unavailable for more than five hours in the last three years."

"Very well, I'll listen to the messages, but unless it's life or death, I'm not calling her back."

Elizabeth had to be content with that. She kissed him on the cheek and curled up beside him as they both listened to the messages on Roark's phone. Several offered congratulations. Roark had given Vance a heads-up on their plans as they'd headed to the airport. Vance must have passed the word along to Roark's friends.

Roark cut off one message from a deep-voiced man named Smith. Elizabeth figured that was the man who was helping Roark with his elusive thief. Ann Richardson's messages progressed from irritation to acute displeasure. Elizabeth winced as Roark deleted the third one.

Ann was heading to Rayas and was pretty upset with Roark for taking off without giving her the statue. She was worried that the negative publicity coming out of Rayas about the missing Gold Heart statue would cause the board to vote to sell the company to Dalton Rothschild. Or worse, with the way the company's stock was plummeting, he might be able to acquire enough stock for a hostile takeover.

The final message had been sent only a few minutes earlier.

"I was at the airport waiting for my flight to Rayas this morning when Interpol stopped me from getting on the plane. They detained me for questioning because your mysterious sheikh's shipment arrived and the Gold Heart statue wasn't part of the cargo. I explained to them that because of all the controversy he'd decided not to sell the statue, but they wouldn't let me leave the country until I produce some sort of proof that his statue isn't the one missing from Rayas. Somehow a reporter caught wind that I was being questioned by Interpol and wrote an article speculating about our recent troubles. Waverly's stock has dropped even further. I need you back in New York and I need that statue. Call me."

Roark's features were set in grim lines as he deleted the message.

"What are you going to do?" Elizabeth asked.

"The same thing I was going to do before her call. I have to get the documents back from Masler before he can give them to Rothschild. It's the only way Rashid will let anyone see his statue and the only way to prove once and for all that it's not the one missing from Rayas's palace."

He tossed the phone onto a nearby chair and rolled Elizabeth onto her back. He threaded his fingers through her damp hair and dusted kisses over her nose, cheeks and eyes.

"But first," he murmured. "I'm going to make love to my wife."

With a heart bursting with love and a broad smile, Elizabeth teased, "I'll bet you never thought you'd hear yourself say those words."

"I think I knew the moment I set eyes on you."

"Really?" Seeing he meant every word, she snuggled closer. "I think I've loved you since the moment you took my hand and asked me if I like to play with new ideas."

He turned her palm up and traced her love line. "The way this curves means you're romantic and passionate."

She chuckled. "Don't you mean foolish when it comes to love?"

"Not at all. See how your head line and your life line start at the same point but separate right away? That means a decisive and determined personality. Someone who can handle adventurous and erratic situations."

"Meaning marriage to you?"

"I promise you'll never be bored."

As Roark's hands skimmed down her sides, Elizabeth reached up to pull his lips to hers. "I never doubted that for a second."

* * * * *

*Turn the page
for a special bonus story
by* USA TODAY *bestselling author
Barbara Dunlop.
Then look for the thrilling conclusion
of THE HIGHEST BIDDER,
A Golden Betrayal,
also by Barbara Dunlop.
Wherever Harlequin Books are sold.*

THE GOLD HEART, PART 5
Barbara Dunlop

Crown Prince Raif Khouri watched his father's chest rise and fall beneath the light blanket in the master chamber of Valhan Palace. The king was battling Partang fever again, the third bout this year. He'd contracted the disease thirty years ago in Eastern Africa. It came and went, but lately it seemed to be taking a greater toll. The king had lost ten pounds in the past month, weight he could ill afford to give up.

"My son." His voice was raspy.

"Yes, Father?" Raif shifted his chair closer, leaning down to listen to his father's faint voice.

"Alber is aligning with the Brazilians."

"I know." Raif nodded. He knew very well the risk the alliance presented to Rayas.

"Kalila must marry the son without delay."

Raif knew that, as well. Every day that passed without a formal betrothal of his cousin to Ari Alber increased their risk of significant financial loss to Rayas. But his headstrong, young cousin, second in line to the throne, had returned from a year of school in Britain with an attitude and the claim of a British boyfriend. Raif could deal with the attitude, but the boyfriend was going to be history. Nothing could interfere with Kalila's duty to the royal family.

"She is stubborn," Raif told the King.

"This is no time for defiance."

"I understand." And Raif was doing everything in his power to bring her into line.

"If we don't act now, Algerian oil will power Moroccan smelters, feeding Indian factories, all financed by Brazilian equity funds and shipped by Greece. We'll be cut out of the deal." The king wasn't saying anything Raif didn't already know.

The thing Raif didn't know was what to do about it. A hundred years ago—hell, fifty years ago—they'd have married Kalila off to Ari Alber, willing or not. Rayas was a shipping nation, a powerhouse in the region. And that meant they had a massive fleet to keep under contract. Kalila's marriage would cement their relationship with the Alber dynasty, which would keep open the doors to Algeria and India.

"The girl must do her duty," said the king.

"I'll talk to her," Raif promised.

"Do more than talk if necessary."

"You would have me beat my own cousin?"

"I would have you threaten to beat her."

Based on his last conversation with Kalila, Raif knew it was going to take more than a simple threat to make her see reason.

"What of Jacx?" the king asked, his spurt of anger-fueled energy clearly flagging.

Raif understood what his father meant by the question. But it was another place where Raif had thus far failed. He chose his words carefully. "When we need Jacx, I will promote him."

"It is not yet done?"

"I offered to make him an admiral." Raif sat back in his chair. It would have been nice if one thing in his life had gone smoothly.

"And?"

"And he prefers to remain a captain."

"What?" The king tried to sit up, but started coughing, racking his chest and turning his face ruddy.

Raif rose to get the doctor, but the king waved him off.

"I am not dying yet," the king wheezed, dropping back down. "Jacx wants to earn his commission. He doesn't want it handed to him because he married Aimee."

Though Jacx's stance on the matter didn't suit Raif's current purpose, he had to admire the man for taking it.

"He did his duty," the king noted with conviction. "He will be rewarded."

"He wanted to marry Aimee." Raif had seen the determination in Jacx's eyes.

Adhering to ancient tradition, Jacx had stepped into the breach five months ago and married Raif's cousin Aimee when the groom had left her at the altar. Jacx had saved the king, Aimee and the royal family from intense embarrassment.

"That proves he's intelligent. Aimee is the best of the lot. Make him an admiral." The king's eyes closed.

"You should sleep, Father."

"What of the Gold Heart?" The king's voice grew fainter, and his puffy eyes remained closed.

"We're still looking." Raif felt his tension rise to new heights as he answered the question.

"Find it," the king ordered. "Find it, and Kalila will cease this nonsense. It's the curse. You know it's the curse."

"Father," Raif sighed.

"You can't deny your history," said the king.

"Folklore is not history." Raif didn't believe for one moment that luck or a cursed statue had anything to do with their current troubles.

"Then explain Salima's death? The demise of that branch of the Bajal dynasty?"

"War, disease and poor judgment," Raif countered.

"Bah," the king scoffed, bringing on another coughing fit.

"Sleep," Raif told him again.

But the king's eyes opened, revealing the determination and intelligence that had allowed him to stay on the throne of a volatile country for nearly thirty years. "I shall not rest until the Gold Heart is home. I dare not."

"Then I will bring it home," Raif vowed, straightening his father's covers.

Cursed or not, the statue would bring peace to his ill father and allay the fears of the Rayasian people. And Raif knew who had stolen the priceless heirloom. He was about to grant Ann Richardson's request and confront her in person.

Though he'd spent two years in Britain at college, it had been a long time since Raif had seen a woman in slacks, her shapely legs and rear end delineated by the soft fabric, indecently so by Rayasian standards.

But out in the garden, Ann Richardson wore a pair of clinging, faded blue jeans set off by high heels and a gleaming copper tank top. Her bare shoulders were creamy smooth, her short hair shimmered blond in the setting sun of the Valhan Palace gardens, while strands of teal beads decorated her neck, and matching earrings dangled from her delicate lobes. He'd seen pictures and knew her skin was honey-pale, eyes jewel-blue. And when she looked in his direction across the garden, he felt an unexpected and unwelcome jolt of arousal.

He reminded himself that this woman was the enemy. She'd taken from the Khouri family one of their most prized possessions.

"You brought her to the palace?" he asked his cousin Tariq, letting the censure come through his tone.

"You agreed to meet her in person," Tariq reminded him.

"I meant at one of the offices downtown. She doesn't deserve to be in the palace." He'd let the woman cool her heels for three days since she'd arrived in Rayas, refusing to grant her a single courtesy.

"Then talk to her in the garden." Impatience was growing in Tariq's tone.

Raif shot him a sharp look.

"Your Royal Highness," Tariq finished, his expression carefully neutral, so that Raif couldn't tell if he was being contrite or sarcastic.

"You forget yourself," Raif admonished.

"I forgot myself a long time ago," Tariq returned.

Raif took one more long look at Ann Richardson, tamped down his inappropriate physical attraction to her, squared his shoulders and exited through the palace archway into the garden.

She watched him unabashed as he followed a winding stone pathway, past date and palm trees. The closer he got, the more beautiful she became. He'd seen many pictures, had her investigated quite thoroughly once he heard she was offering up his statue for sale. But nothing he'd seen had done her justice. She was quite simply the most stunningly beautiful woman he'd ever laid eyes on.

"Miss Richardson," he greeted without inflection.

"Prince Raif," she answered in return. No bow or curtsy. Perhaps Americans didn't acknowledge royalty. The British did, though reluctantly if one wasn't a member of the Windsor royal family. Still, there was some acknowledgment from them that he wasn't a stable hand. Not so from Ann Richardson.

They were both standing, and he left it that way. The sun was dipping below the horizon, and he had a busy night ahead. Better to get this over with.

"You are here to confess?" he asked. It was the only acceptable outcome from his perspective.

She gave a throaty chuckle that seemed to strum along his nervous system, reigniting his arousal. "Hardly."

"Then you're wasting my time." He turned to go.

"Wait. Prince Raif." Her hand touched his arm.

He turned sharply and glared at her serious breach of protocol.

"I'm here to explain."

If he thought her looks had aroused him, and that her voice had made the feelings more acute, her touch was threatening to push him over the edge.

"I would advise you to remove your hand," he told her.

She stilled. Her expression faltered.

"My guards are watching, and you are forbidden from touching a royal."

The guards were the least of his worries. His flesh burned under her touch, and his mind was filled with visions of dragging her into his arms and ravishing her lithe body.

Her eyes widening at his expression, she pulled back her hand. "You were about to walk away," she explained.

"There's no point in my staying."

"I've come a long way to make you see reason."

"You mean you've come a long way to lie."

"I'm not here to lie. There are two statues. Waverly's is not selling yours."

Raif didn't believe her for a second. If Waverly's had truly discovered Princess Salima's missing statue, they would prove it. "If you're not here to confess, then you're here to lie."

"I'm here to help."

Raif was growing impatient with her cute words. "I could have you thrown in jail."

"How would that help?"

It was a fair question. It wouldn't help at all. "It would give me a great deal of satisfaction."

"But it wouldn't get your statue back."

"If you give back the statue, I won't throw you in jail."

Her blue eyes narrowed as if his words had momentarily thrown her. But she recovered quickly. "I thought we could compare notes."

Raif widened his stance, crossing his arms over his chest. He'd give her about ten seconds more. She might be beautiful, and the sound of her voice might send desire flaring up his spine, but that didn't mean he was going to stand here and let her waste his time.

"You tell me what you know," she continued. "I'll tell you what I know. Perhaps between the two of us, we can figure out what really happened."

It was Raif's turn to chuckle, and she had the good grace to blush—very easy to see with that pale skin of hers.

"So you can distract me?" he taunted. "Feed me false information and send me in the wrong direction?"

"I'm not going—"

"I'm not that gullible, Miss Richardson."

"Ms."

"Ms.," he enunciated, drawing out the sound. "I'm not that gullible."

"I'm here to help."

He didn't believe that for one second.

"This is messing up my life, too, you know," she told him.

"In what way?" he demanded, losing his usual iron grip on his temper. "Because Waverly's will make a fortune? Because you'll get a fat commission? My father is gravely ill. My sister is wreaking havoc on the family honor. My navy needs a new admiral. A multi-billion dollar trade deal is about to blow up in my face. And I'm wasting valuable time chasing after a priceless heirloom. But, please, do tell me how this is messing up your life?"

Ann set her jaw. "Your accusations are destroying my professional reputation. When this is all over, you'll still be the Crown Prince, but I'll be out of a job."

So, there was going to be some small consequence for her actions. It was hollow comfort. "You should have thought of that before you stole my statue."

"I did not—"

"This is getting us nowhere."

The sun had fully set now, and traditional, evening horns sounded in the distance. Torches were being lit in the garden near the palace, but Raif and Ann were in a dark corner.

She moved close to him, her voice lowering. "I agree. You are wasting your time. If you chase me, the real thief will get away."

"If I chase you?" His voice rose. "If? I *am* chasing you, Ann. And I'm going to catch you. And when I do, you are going to be held accountable for the grief you have caused my family."

She considered him for a long moment. "Why am I picturing dank dungeons and gruel?"

It took him a moment to realize she was mocking him. She

doubted the extent of his power? This was his country. He could have her thrown in jail with the wave of one hand.

He leaned in, affecting his most imperious tone of voice. "Tread carefully, Ann."

But she didn't back off. "Your statue is gone, Prince Raif. And I'm innocent. This is my one and only offer to help you. Take it or leave it."

He could smell her now, vanilla, intoxicating. And he was drawn into those crystal blue eyes. The urge to haul her into his arms was overpowering. Haul her into his arms and do what, he asked himself? Shake her? Throttle her? Kiss her?

It was to kiss her, he admitted to himself. And he sure didn't want to stop there.

Her voice turned to a whisper, her breath sweet against his own. "Take it or leave it, Raif."

He took it. But it wasn't what she was expecting.

He had a fleeting glimpse of her surprised gasp, before his lips came down on hers. His arm went around her waist, jerking her tight against an instantaneous erection.

She pushed against his shoulders, struggling to speak.

But he didn't back off. His kiss was carnal and determined. He overwhelmed her mouth, his tongue assailing the seam of her lips. His free hand plunged into her hair, fingering its satin smoothness, trapping her against his mouth.

Then her hands stopped pushing, and her lips went pliant. She opened to let him in.

When her tongue tangled with his, fireworks ignited his brain stem, sizzling their way to the top of his skull. Her body molded against his, and he braced himself, letting soft meet hard.

Her lips were parted, and she was kissing him back. A whimper sounded deep in her throat. She wasn't fighting, not that it had actually occurred to him to care. Well, not until this second, when he remembered who they were and what was between them, and now he knew he'd have to bring things under control.

But not yet.

For a stolen moment longer, he was going to let this passion race between them. He wrapped his arms fully around her, coupling their bodies together, pretending it didn't have to end. Her own arms went around his neck, pulling the little tank top, revealing a strip of her bare skin at her midriff.

He ran his fingertips along the warm softness. She shivered, and he bent her backward, boldly running his hands beneath her top, stroking her flat stomach, trailing his thumbs below the mound of her breasts.

"Prince Raif," she gasped, and the sound of his own name arced his arousal.

He kissed her temple, her ear, the curve of her neck. One hand explored her bare skin, while the other cupped her bottom, holding her firmly against the driving need of his body.

She pressed her forehead against his shoulder, still squeezing him tight, drawing deep, labored breaths. "We have to stop."

His mind screamed no, but he forced his hands to still.

"Right," he agreed on a strained gasp.

"This isn't getting us anywhere," she rasped.

That wasn't strictly true. But it was getting Raif a whole lot of places he didn't dare go.

He'd never lost control like this. His sex life was carefully orchestrated, planned, executed. But Ann had gotten under his skin in a way that was dangerous. Especially considering who she was.

How had he forgotten who she was?

He drew back, steeling himself. "I hope you didn't think to use your body to change my mind."

She blinked at him. "You kissed me, remember?"

"To put you in your place." At least that was how it had started. "But you took the opportunity quickly enough."

"Is that the way things work in Rayas? When a woman stands her ground, you accost her?"

Raif wanted to laugh at Ann's protest. She'd been an enthusiastic participant in the kiss, and they both knew it.

"I'm the crown prince," he drawled, refusing to either defend or explain. "If that's the way I want things to work, that's the way they work."

"You have absolute power?"

"Absolutely."

They stared at each other in silence for a long moment.

He was dying to kiss her again. But he did possess some self-control. Though it had been tested.

"Go back to America, Ann," he told her. "Either give me my statue, or go back to America. This ruse you've concocted about helping me is not going to work. I don't know what you're up to, but I can guarantee you, I am going to find out the truth."

"Good." Her gaze stayed steady on his. "You do that, Raif. You find out the truth. And when you do, I'll expect an apology." She eyed him up and down. "For the false accusation. For the unwanted kiss, and for anything else you manage to do between now and then."

Before she could move, he grasped her chin. "If you don't want a kiss, Ms. Richardson, you might want to keep your tongue to yourself."

She held her ground without pulling back. "You took me by surprise."

Surprise was putting it mildly from Raif's perspective. "And if you don't want me as an enemy," he continued his warning, mentally blocking the kiss, "you might want to stop defying me."

"Your threats don't frighten me."

"Really?" he drawled. "You'd be the first."

COMING NEXT MONTH from Harlequin Desire®
AVAILABLE NOVEMBER 27, 2012

#2197 ONE WINTER'S NIGHT
The Westmorelands
Brenda Jackson
Riley Westmoreland never mixes business with pleasure—until he meets his company's gorgeous new party planner and realizes one night will never be enough.

#2198 A GOLDEN BETRAYAL
The Highest Bidder
Barbara Dunlop
The head of a New York auction house is swept off her feet by the crown prince of a desert kingdom who has accused her of trafficking in stolen goods!

#2199 STAKING HIS CLAIM
Billionaires and Babies
Tessa Radley
She never planned a baby...he doesn't plan to let his baby go. The solution should be simple. But no one told Ella that love is the riskiest business of all....

#2200 BECOMING DANTE
The Dante Legacy
Day Leclaire
Gabe Moretti discovers he's not just a Moretti—he's a secret Dante. Now the burning passion—the Inferno—for Kat Malloy won't be ignored....

#2201 THE SHEIKH'S DESTINY
Desert Knights
Olivia Gates
Marrying Laylah is Rashid's means to the throne. But when she discovers his plot and casts him from her heart, will claiming the throne mean anything if he loses her?

#2202 THE DEEPER THE PASSION...
The Drummond Vow
Jennifer Lewis
When Vicki St. Cyr is forced to ask the man who broke her heart for help in claiming a reward, old passions and long-buried emotions flare.

You can find more information on upcoming Harlequin® titles, free excerpts and more at www.Harlequin.com.

HDCNM1112

REQUEST YOUR FREE BOOKS!
2 FREE NOVELS PLUS 2 FREE GIFTS!

❧ Harlequin®

Desire

ALWAYS POWERFUL, PASSIONATE AND PROVOCATIVE

YES! Please send me 2 FREE Harlequin Desire® novels and my 2 FREE gifts (gifts are worth about $10). After receiving them, if I don't wish to receive any more books, I can return the shipping statement marked "cancel." If I don't cancel, I will receive 6 brand-new novels every month and be billed just $4.30 per book in the U.S. or $4.99 per book in Canada. That's a saving of at least 14% off the cover price! It's quite a bargain! Shipping and handling is just 50¢ per book in the U.S. and 75¢ per book in Canada.* I understand that accepting the 2 free books and gifts places me under no obligation to buy anything. I can always return a shipment and cancel at any time. Even if I never buy another book, the two free books and gifts are mine to keep forever.

225/326 HDN FEF3

Name	(PLEASE PRINT)

Address	Apt. #

City	State/Prov.	Zip/Postal Code

Signature (if under 18, a parent or guardian must sign)

Mail to the **Reader Service:**
IN U.S.A.: P.O. Box 1867, Buffalo, NY 14240-1867
IN CANADA: P.O. Box 609, Fort Erie, Ontario L2A 5X3

Not valid for current subscribers to Harlequin Desire books.

Want to try two free books from another line?
Call 1-800-873-8635 or visit www.ReaderService.com.

* Terms and prices subject to change without notice. Prices do not include applicable taxes. Sales tax applicable in N.Y. Canadian residents will be charged applicable taxes. Offer not valid in Quebec. This offer is limited to one order per household. All orders subject to credit approval. Credit or debit balances in a customer's account(s) may be offset by any other outstanding balance owed by or to the customer. Please allow 4 to 6 weeks for delivery. Offer available while quantities last.

Your Privacy—The Reader Service is committed to protecting your privacy. Our Privacy Policy is available online at www.ReaderService.com or upon request from the Reader Service.

We make a portion of our mailing list available to reputable third parties that offer products we believe may interest you. If you prefer that we not exchange your name with third parties, or if you wish to clarify or modify your communication preferences, please visit us at www.ReaderService.com/consumerchoice or write to us at Reader Service Preference Service, P.O. Box 9062, Buffalo, NY 14269. Include your complete name and address.

HDES11B

Harlequin® Desire is proud to present

ONE WINTER'S NIGHT

by New York Times *bestselling author*

Brenda Jackson

Alpha Blake tightened her coat around her. Not only would she be late for her appointment with Riley Westmoreland, but because of her flat tire they would have to change the location of the meeting and Mr. Westmoreland would be the one driving her there. This was totally embarrassing, when she had been trying to make a good impression.

She turned up the heat in her car. Even with a steady stream of hot air coming in through the car vents, she still felt cold, too cold, and wondered if she would ever get used to the Denver weather. Of course, it was too late to think about that now. It was her first winter here, and she didn't have any choice but to grin and bear it. When she'd moved, she'd felt that getting as far away from Daytona Beach as she could was essential to her peace of mind. But who in her right mind would prefer blistering-cold Denver to sunny Daytona Beach? Only a person wanting to start a new life and put a painful past behind her.

Her attention was snagged by an SUV that pulled off the road and parked in front of her. The door swung open and long denim-clad, boot-wearing legs appeared before a man stepped out of the truck. She met his gaze through the windshield and forgot to breathe. Walking toward her car was a man who was so dangerously masculine, so heart-stoppingly virile, that her brain went momentarily numb.

He was tall, and the Stetson on his head made him appear taller. But his height was secondary to the sharp handsomeness of his features.

Her gaze slid all over him as he moved his long limbs toward her vehicle in a walk that was so agile and self-assured, she envied the confidence he exuded with every step. Her breasts suddenly peaked, and she could actually feel blood rushing through her veins.

She didn't have to guess who this man was.

He was Riley Westmoreland.

Find out if Riley and Alpha mix business with pleasure in

ONE WINTER'S NIGHT

by Brenda Jackson

Available December 2012

Only from Harlequin® Desire

SPECIAL EDITION

Life, Love and Family

NEW YORK TIMES BESTSELLING AUTHOR

DIANA PALMER

brings you a brand-new Western romance
featuring characters that readers have come to
love—the Brannt family from Harlequin HQN's
bestselling book *WYOMING TOUGH*.

Cort Brannt, Texas rancher through and through,
is about to unexpectedly get lassoed by love!

THE RANCHER

Available November 13 wherever books are sold!

Also available as a 2-in-1
THE RANCHER & HEART OF STONE

www.Harlequin.com

HSE65709DP

Harlequin *Desire*

ALWAYS POWERFUL, PASSIONATE AND PROVOCATIVE.

**DON'T MISS THE SEDUCTIVE CONCLUSION
TO THE MINISERIES**

THE HIGHEST BIDDER

WITH FAN-FAVORITE AUTHOR

BARBARA DUNLOP

Prince Raif Khouri believes that Waverly's
high-end-auction-house executive Ann Richardson
is responsible for the theft of his valuable antique Gold
Heart statue, rumored to be a good luck charm to his
family. The only way Raif can keep an eye on her—
and get the truth from her—is by kidnapping Ann and
taking her to his kingdom. But soon Raif finds himself
the prisoner as Ann tempts him like no one else.

A GOLDEN BETRAYAL

Available December 2012 from Harlequin® Desire.

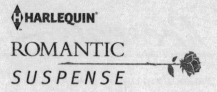

HARLEQUIN®

ROMANTIC
SUSPENSE

Get your heart racing this holiday season with double the pulse-pounding action.

Christmas Confidential

Featuring

Holiday Protector by **Marilyn Pappano**

Miri Duncan doesn't care that it's almost Christmas. She's got bigger worries on her mind. But surviving the trip to Georgia from Texas is going to be her biggest challenge. Days in a car with the man who broke her heart and helped send her to prison—private investigator Dean Montgomery.

A Chance Reunion by **Linda Conrad**

When the husband Elana Novak left behind five years ago shows up in her new California home she knows danger is coming her way. To protect the man she is quickly falling for Elana must convince private investigator Gage Chance that she is a different person. But Gage isn't about to let her walk away...even with the bad guys right on their heels.

Available December 2012 wherever books are sold!

www.Harlequin.com

HRS27801